CODE LIGHTFALL

AND THE
ROBOT KING

DANIEL H. WILSON

BLOOMSBURY

LONDON BERLIN NEW YORK SYDNEY

Bloomsbury Publishing, London, Berlin, New York and Sydney

First published in Great Britain in February 2011
by Bloomsbury Publishing Plc
36 Soho Square, London, W1D 3QY

First published in the USA in January 2011
by Bloomsbury Books for Young Readers
175 Fifth Avenue, New York, NY 10010

ISBN 978 1 4088 1419 2

Printed in Great Britain by Clays Ltd, St Ives plc, Bungay, Suffolk

1 3 5 7 9 10 8 6 4 2
www.bloomsbury.com

For Cora

Contents

CODE
LIGHTFALL
AND THE
ROBOT KING

1

Mek Mound

[Traverse Complete]
[Three]
[Two]
[One]
[Activate]
[Once Upon a Time . . .]

. . . there was a boy named Code Lightfall who was very, very shy.

No matter what the situation, Code found that the safest course of action was usually to take no action at all. Instead, he preferred to simply imagine all of the possible outcomes— right up until one of them happened.

It didn't help that his name was, well, weird. When Code asked his parents where it came from, they would only say that it was special. Code's name had been passed down through the Lightfall family for generations, but it hadn't made it any easier to make friends. The problem was that the name Code rhymed with too many regrettable words, such as toad, load and à la mode. Since Code was skinny and shy and had a funny name, he had learned that it was better to stay away from other kids, especially the bigger ones. Over the years, he had become an expert at keeping his head down and his mouth shut.

On this particular day, Code was sitting alone in his usual spot in the front row of the school bus. He pushed his unruly black hair away from his eyes and stared out of the open window. The air outside was muggy and heavy. Heat lightning flickered silently inside bruised clouds, but no rain fell. All around him, the other kids were talking and joking and jumping around in the seats. With every deep rumble of thunder, they squealed and laughed. But Code was quiet, as usual.

This was the last field trip on the last day of sixth grade.

A minute later, the bus skidded to a stop in a dusty car park. The instant the bus door wheezed open, Code ducked down the steps and out.

There weren't many places to go on field trips where Code was from, and he had been to this one many times—Mek Mound. Code was standing at the foot of a hilly pyramid that rose majestically from the Great Plains of eastern Oklahoma. Code had read that the mounds were built thousands of years before the Egyptian pyramids and had once been covered with temples and fortresses. But those were all gone. Now Code saw only centuries-old oak trees and waving grass. Mek Mound looked like an emerald green mountain plopped down in the flat middle of nowhere.

Up until last summer, the mounds had been Code's favourite place in the world because he used to visit them with his grandfather. John Lightfall was a quiet Cherokee man who often had a sly smile on his face—as if he knew the punch line to the world's greatest joke. The two of them would walk the mound together, not talking much, just exploring. The place didn't attract many visitors, but Code always felt as if he were being watched. His grandfather used to say that Code was feeling the spirits of their ancestors, lingering on in this ancient place.

And then one day last year, John Lightfall visited Mek Mound alone and never came back. The police looked into his disappearance, but they never discovered a thing. John Lightfall was here and then he was just gone.

Now far-off thunder grumbled and a warm breeze pushed Code's hair into his eyes.

A colourful confusion of students piled out of the bus behind him, carrying backpacks and lunch boxes.

"A big pile of earth. How *interesting*," said Tyler, narrowing his cat-like eyes as he shoved Code out of the way.

From the corner of his eye, Code saw Hazel emerge from the bus. She was lanky and had chewed fingernails and the sun always seemed to be in her hair. Once at breaktime he had watched her catch a bee in her hands and then let it go. He remembered being impressed that she wasn't even a little bit afraid of getting stung. Even though they'd been in school together since nursery, the two had never been able to look at each other; their eyes always seemed to slide away like butter on a hot pan. Today was no different.

Finally, the teacher, Mr Mefford, hopped out of the bus. He looked warily at the billowing clouds, then addressed the class.

"Mound builders," said Mr Mefford, "are the ancestors of modern-day Native Americans. There are thousands of these mounds spread all over North America, from New York to Oklahoma. Nobody knows exactly what their purpose was, but Mek Mound is one of the biggest. Now, I want everyone to visit each part of the mound, read the plaques and fill out your worksheets. We'll meet back here for lunch, and afterwards there *will* be a quiz."

The students groaned.

Code glanced down at his worksheet. He had already doodled on it. Most of the page was taken up by a drawing of a hulking robot with long, crane-like arms, cannons for fingers and a big smile on its face. Underneath he had written, "Atomic Slaughterbot."

"Ooh, robots!" Tyler laughed, trying to snatch the drawing.

Code stuffed it into his pocket, then turned and walked away towards the mound.

"That's what I thought," said Tyler. "Code the toad. Always hopping away. Here, let me help."

Code felt a push from behind and fell to his knees on the mud.

Code looked up to see Hazel watching. She had been talking to a friend and now stood looking at him, a little frown on her face. Not knowing what else to do, Code got to his feet and hurried up the steep face of the mound. He kept his eyes on the ground and didn't look back.

Why bother fighting? It was easier to do nothing. If he could blend in and disappear maybe the bullies would forget he even existed.

But these worries evaporated as Code began to explore the mound. Under the churning, greenish sky, the colours seemed more vivid and Mek Mound felt alive. Code knew that somewhere deep inside, entwined with gnarled roots, were the bones of nameless kings from ages past—the once powerful rulers of a civilisation that had disappeared. And when the prehistoric builders who created Mek Mound had gone, this sacred place had waited, weathering thousands of years of neglect and emptiness as nature tried to reclaim it.

But nature had failed.

Mek Mound was still here after all this time. *My ancestors built these mounds*, thought Code. *But why?*

Code's grandfather had tried his hardest to find out. John Lightfall had been an anthropologist and spent his entire life studying the mounds. The spry old man had a special knack for spotting hidden possibilities. He used to sit and muse out loud, starting every sentence with the words "What if?" Code smiled, remembering how his grandfather's wise face would wrinkle up in deep thought as he turned an old arrowhead over and over in his rough hands.

After his grandfather's disappearance, Code had tried to stay hopeful. Investigators found his grandfather's car parked at the mound and his satchel near an old oak tree. But as the days and weeks passed and the investigators found no new clues, Code began to lose hope. He chose to stay in his room, reading. His father would shake his head and say, "Get your nose out of that book." His mother would put her hands on her hips and ask, "Why don't you go out and try to make some friends?" Only one person had ever seemed to understand Code, and *he* had gone missing while exploring this place.

Grandpa knew this mound as well as he knew my face, thought Code as he looked around at the waving grass. He couldn't have got lost. Code's grandfather had often said that the mound-builder civilisation was more advanced than modern people thought. *What if?* thought Code. *What if my grandpa wasn't kidnapped, or had an accident, or something so* normal? *What if his disappearance has something to do with the mounds?*

Code began to feverishly speculate. *Could the mounds be linked together? What if my grandpa stood here and was teleported to another mound on the other side of the world? Or what if it's space travel? This could be some sort of launchpad.* Code watched the heavens, imagining a spacecraft levitating there.

Or maybe this mound is just a big pile of earth, thought Code.

After a few seconds, fat raindrops began to fall from the sky. A gentle whoosh of warm wind swept over the mound as the clouds finally released their pent-up cargo. Code heard the other kids whooping and laughing in the sudden downpour. But Code stood still. Something was wrong. He inhaled the smell of wet pavement and grass and kept watching the sky. Strangely, the drops of rain around him seemed to be rising *up* instead of falling down. Code held out his palm. It remained dry.

This can't be happening, thought Code.

Then, as quickly as it had started, the rain shower stopped. Code looked in wonder at the dry grass. Above, the seething clouds flickered with lightning: red, yellow, green and blue. Distantly, he could hear Mr Mefford calling everyone back to the bus. Then a sudden deafening crack of thunder tore across the mound. Code flinched and covered his ears, and did a double take as something caught his eye.

A dark speck. It zoomed across the sky, made a wide, wobbly loop, then swooped down towards the mound. It sped closer and closer, then blew past Code's face, inches away. Code blinked—and it was gone.

This is crazy, thought Code. *Am I dreaming?*

Just then, Code heard a soft sound: *Peep.*

Something had landed on a nearby tree limb. It looked

like a hummingbird and seemed to be cleaning itself. But it wasn't a bird . . . It was smaller and metal. And it was *glowing*. Code looked around for somebody else, anybody, so he could point it out. Some of his classmates were trudging down the hill towards the bus, through the trees. But before he could call out, the speck zipped off once again.

Code caught sight of it further down the hill, hovering in front of Hazel. She was reading a plaque and didn't seem to notice it at all, not even when it shot a quick burst of green light at her face.

It was definitely *not* a bird. Birds weren't made of metal and they didn't shoot beams of light. This thing was unlike any creature Code had ever seen or read about.

And it didn't stop with Hazel; it flitted from student to student, shooting flashes at everyone.

Peep, it said.

The flash didn't seem to do anything, and just like Hazel, none of the other kids noticed it.

Peep. Zachary.

Peep. Tyler.

Peep. Addison.

And now the speck was coming towards him. Realising that he was going to be next, Code held his backpack in front of his face.

And . . . nothing.

Code lowered the backpack, just enough to take one small peek.

Peep.

The light hit Code directly between the eyes and he quickly slapped a hand to his forehead. But the beam didn't hurt. In fact, it sort of tickled. The speck peeped again and accelerated in a wavering, chaotic route until it settled directly on to Code's arm. Its little feet felt cool, and they dimpled his skin—the small creature was heavier than it looked.

It peeped twice, flexed its wings, then rose to hover directly in front of Code's face.

Cross-eyed and trying to focus, Code inspected the intricate little device: it *was* metallic, with a set of blurred wings and tiny, swivelling camera eyes. It glowed a curious green. When Code reached for it, the tiny creature easily dodged away.

It was like some kind of mechanical bumblebee.

Every time Code blinked, he had to search for the speck again. But then something else began to happen. Code's vision slid out of focus and everything became muddled. He shut his eyes for a second, hoping to regroup. Instead, he saw cascading waves of purple and red on the backs of his eyelids. The muggy air, the fluttering noises of grasshoppers and the far-off sound of Mr Mefford's deep voice calling to the kids began to lull him. His head seemed heavy. He felt as though he were falling into the purple and red colours as they mixed and unmixed.

"What's happening?!" whispered Code, forcing his eyes open.

The bee-thing was still hovering in front of him. It buzzed around his head once, flashed red and gave his earlobe a sharp yank.

"Hey!" yelped Code, rubbing his ear.

The bee chirped and flew over the hill. Still feeling dazed, Code followed it, keeping his eyes locked on the buzzing creature so that it wouldn't disappear. It travelled up the overgrown mound, and Code caught up just in time to see the green light dart into a dark hollow in the base of a great oak tree.

Code froze. The hair on the back of his neck was standing on end. This was the exact spot where investigators had found his grandfather's satchel.

Code slung his backpack on to the ground, dropped to all fours and carefully poked his head inside the tree hollow.

Darkness. Code inhaled the cool, damp air. There was a faint roar of wind in the distance, as if he were inside a seashell. As his eyes adjusted, Code was surprised to see that the narrow gouge in the tree opened up into a larger space. Somehow, the empty space inside the tree seemed larger than the tree itself.

Just then, the dark tree hollow began to pulse with a greenish glow. The bee had settled on the far side of the trunk and it gave a sharp chirp that echoed dully in the cramped space.

Code hesitated, a little afraid. Focusing on the spot of

light, he crawled inside. He pulled his knees to his chest and leaned back against the wall. Outside, the rain fell in fat drops that made the grass twitch.

"What are you trying to tell me?" he asked the tiny creature.

The spot of light hopped off the wall and landed on Code's folded arms, casting a warm radiance on his face. He smiled at the strange little creature and shook his head, perplexed. In response, the bee made a singsong peeping noise and flashed blue. It seemed to Code a melancholy colour. Code cocked his head, trying to understand.

"Is something wrong?" asked Code.

Suddenly, the ground beneath him collapsed. For an instant, Code saw the grey crescent of light leading outside, and then everything was swallowed by wet earth, snaking roots and disintegrating leaves. He scrambled to grab something to stop his slide, but it was no use. Code tumbled head over heels in a flurry of slimy leaves and broken bark. He could only squeeze his eyes shut and hope for the best as mud filled his ears, nose and mouth.

After a few long seconds, Code slammed into solid ground. For an agonising moment, he lay there choking and coughing. He could feel cool stone underneath his body. Finally, he sat up and wiped his eyes and nose. Whimpering, he brushed mud out of his hair and off of his clothes. Then he forced himself to take a deep breath. *Don't be scared*, he told himself. *Being scared isn't going to help.* After a few more deep breaths, Code realised that his eyes were still squeezed tightly shut. He opened them slowly.

The glowing bee sat a few feet away. It was a welcome pool of light in the terrifying blackness. And it seemed to be waiting for him. Now it hopped a few inches further down the tunnel, as if beckoning Code to follow.

Code found that he was able to stand up. He put his hands out and touched rough stone walls. Reaching over his head, Code couldn't feel a ceiling. With all his might, he jumped straight up, fingers outstretched. He felt nothing. The walls were bumpy, but not enough to get a grip. *I can't climb back out*, he thought. Looking up, he could see nothing but darkness.

"Help!" he shouted. "Hello?!"

His voice was muffled by the earth and rock. It was like shouting with a pillow held over his face.

To make things worse, the glowing bee was flying further away down the tunnel, its comforting green light getting dimmer. *Nobody is going to hear me*, Code thought. *And without light, I'll never find my way out of here.* He crept forward, concentrating on the dot of light as it darted ahead another few inches.

"Hold on," he whispered. "Hey, stop for a second!"

But the glowing speck flittered up to chest height and dived a little further into the tunnel. Code had to creep faster and faster to keep up. Little by little, the creature accelerated until it was a streak of light, zipping up and down and over and around in the darkness.

"Wait!" called Code. He walked, then trotted, then sprinted until he could barely breathe. At one point, his lunch money fell out of his trouser pocket. He could have sworn that he was running on the ceiling, upside down.

Finally, Code saw a faint light—the tunnel's end: *I must be all the way back to the school bus*, he thought with relief. Code wished that he could have shared this with his grandfather. Who would have guessed that there were tunnels running through the mound?

Code stopped just short of the pale grey light coming in from a jagged crevice in the wall. The little creature fluttered over to him and briefly touched its tiny face to his cheek. Then it landed on his outstretched hand and peeped, flashing a beam of light towards the tunnel exit, as if urging Code to step outside.

Code paused, hesitant.

The bee purred and flashed to a bluish colour, then quickly turned back to gold. Code was starting to figure out his small companion: blue meant sad and gold meant happy. Cupped in his palm, the mysterious creature was glowing gold and seemed very excited.

"He needs a name," said Code, to nobody in particular. "How about I call him Peep?" In response, the tiny creature hopped into the air and wheeled around. It shot Code with a red light beam and lightly pinched his forearm.

"OK, OK," said Code, rubbing his arm. "What I *meant* to say is I think I'll call *her* Peep."

This seemed to be better.

Peep blinked a cheerful golden colour and darted out of the tunnel. Wiping sweat from his forehead, Code took a deep breath and followed her outside.

2

The Odd Woods

Code peeked his head out of the crack in the rock wall and did not see a road, a school bus, or a thunderstorm. From the instant knot in his stomach, Code knew that he was definitely, without a doubt, utterly and completely lost. Swallowing, he looked up at the twisting, vine-encrusted trees that towered overhead. He had never seen trees like this at Mek Mound before.

Peep, a green dot of light, flew a few feet ahead, swooping through the air like a firefly on a mission. She was the only familiar sight. Code hesitantly followed her, trudging into the dim forest.

Something is wrong with this place, he thought. A mournful, hushed feeling filled the woods. Code noticed that the muted shadows of leaves on the forest floor were perfectly still. The trees didn't sway, not even a little. The leaves didn't chatter to each other the way they did on Mek Mound. He could hear a breeze whistling through the branches above, but the moss-covered tree limbs still hung motionless, like carved statues.

It was eerie, but Code was curious. Besides, Peep was happily pouncing from tree to tree. Reassured by the steady drone of Peep's wings, Code turned his attention to investigating the woods around him.

Hearing a peculiar *criiick, criiick* coming from a deep cluster of bushes, Code pushed aside a stiff patch of tall grass and saw a squat brown toad. Carefully, Code scooped up the little creature only to find that it was some kind of clockwork toad, hard and bumpy and heavy, with a winder jutting out of its side. It gave a sharp mechanical kick of its legs and escaped into the bushes.

Hurrying to catch up with Peep, Code noticed an intricate silver spider's web hanging from a tree branch. It seemed to hum softly in the shadows, like a sputtering neon sign. A metallic lump with long, splintery legs—the spider, Code realised—hung from a springy wire. As Code passed by, a translucent gnat landed on the web and was barbecued with a *zap*.

What a strange place this is, Code thought. Everything was different here, from the leaves to the animals. Nothing was natural. Everything was made of metal or plastic or glass.

Looking around in wonder, Code stepped over waist-high roots and ducked under low-hanging branches. He stopped and ran his fingers over an oddly solid tree trunk. The bark didn't crumble at all. "Peep, is this whole place full of robots just like you? Even the *trees* are made of metal."

Peep winked a happy orange, then went back to curious green as she kept gliding forward through the gloom.

A pang of fear ran through Code when he realised that he could no longer see the tunnel entrance. He didn't know the way back to the tunnel. But come to think of it, he didn't know the way back from the tunnel to the mound either. *Not only do I not know the way back*, he thought. *I don't know the way back from the way back.* So Code decided to do the only rational thing: go forward.

After a few more minutes of walking, Code stopped in his tracks. Before him was a thing that he absolutely could not make sense of. It was a shiny wall. No . . . it was a swiftly flowing silver brook. Wait—it was a blur of speeding sticks. Code squinted at the bizarre sight—it was like trying to focus on the spinning blades of a ceiling fan. No. It couldn't be. Were those . . . legs? The more he looked, the more Code became sure: it was a thousand pairs of connected legs running almost but not quite faster than Code could see. The running wall was taller than Code and connected to a long, grey centipede-like body. It stretched through the woods in both directions as far as he could see.

Peep kept going, flying right over the top.

"Wait!" shouted Code. He hopped up and down in vain, trying to see over the speeding wall. "Oh, Peep," he muttered. For a few minutes, he searched for a way round but found nothing. Finally, Code sat down on a glinting rock and rested his chin in his hand.

He was starting to feel really afraid. Alone in a strange, motionless forest filled with robotic animals—and now this, a metal wall of legs violently hurtling past. The shining barrier kicked up a breeze that ruffled his hair. *I just need to get past this wall,* he thought. *Peep is the only one who seems to know the way. I'll find her and then get out of here,* he promised himself. Back to the mound and the school bus and home.

Code picked up a stick and slowly held it out towards the silvery blur of motion. *Crack!* It was smashed to splinters the instant it made contact. Code dropped the broken stick and rubbed his bruised hand. Touching this thing would break his arm, he realised. And it was too high to jump over, even if he climbed a tree. Code looked to the left and right again. The wall didn't seem to have a beginning or end. Feeling small and alone, Code turned away from the wall and looked back the way he had come, wishing desperately that Peep would return so he didn't have to figure this out by himself.

Then Code felt a tap on his shoulder.

"That was very rude," said a broad, insectile face with quivering antennae. "Even for a brute living in the Odd Woods."

A jolt of fear and surprise raced through Code, but he couldn't react. It was all he could do to keep breathing. A smooth metallic face with emerald green bug eyes loomed over him. When it spoke, two sharp mandibles clacked back and forth in its mouth, like serrated knives.

"Well?" asked the creature. "Haven't you got anything to say?"

Code gasped in wonder as he realised the face was connected to the centipede-like body that curved off into the distance. This creature *was* the silver wall! The moving wall of legs slowed down and finally stopped. One slim leg reached up and scratched its belly, just like a cat.

"I'm sorry," said Code, studying the insect's face. It seemed very odd that this monstrous thing from who knows where should speak perfect English.

"I was just . . ." Code trailed off.

"Experimenting?"

"I didn't know that you were. I mean—" Code pointed at the row of tall, thin legs. "This is all *you*?" he asked.

"Right. I'm an infinipede, thanks. And I'm sorry if I startled you, but your nasty poke with that stick makes us quite even. Maybe more so."

"Where am I? What is this place?" implored Code.

"What a silly question. You're in Mekhos, obviously. The land of the robots. And if you don't mind, I'll be off now."

The answer made no sense, but the mysterious creature was already preparing to race away into the murky woods.

"Wait," pleaded Code. "I'm not from here. I'm . . . lost. I need to know where this place is so that I can get back home."

The infinipede clattered its mandibles together, chuckling at him. "My dear little brute. Mekhos is exactly where it is supposed to be. Nowhere else. As everyone knows, our pocket of reality was carved out of space and time ages ago."

"What do you mean? By who?"

"The ancient titans. The mound builders. You know, *humans.*"

"Humans?" Code repeated.

"Yes, yes. Humans are a race of monsters as tall as trees and stronger than the currents of the Mercurial River. They created Mekhos as a laboratory. A big experiment. You may not know it, brute, but you are an experiment out of control. We all are."

Code's mind raced. The mound builders! They made this place as an experiment? What kind of experiment needed a whole new world as a laboratory?

"But why?" Code breathed.

"I suppose the humans built Mekhos for us because we are so terribly . . . dangerous. Best for them if we keep our worlds separate. Don't leave the peace of the Odd Woods, little brute. There are things out there that would make you wish you didn't have sensors. Horrors as big as the sky that can crush you into bits and pieces. And there are other fiends. Nanoscopic creatures, smaller than dust, that will make you wish you'd never been invented. They can wriggle through your outer casing and tear you apart from the inside. Trust me, Mekhos can be a very *nasty* place."

All of a sudden a thought occurred to Code: *Maybe my grandfather came here, too.* If anyone had seen the old man, it would be this long creature that seemed to be everywhere at once. Barely daring to hope, Code asked, "Have you *seen* any humans?"

The infinipede sighed.

"Alas, the ancients made us, gave us our programs and then abandoned us. Nobody has seen a human being for thousands of years."

Code's shoulders slumped. No luck.

"All except for the one, of course," added the infinipede.

Code arched his eyebrows questioningly.

"How ignorant can you be?" asked the infinipede. "I'm speaking of His Excellency, the King of the Greater Mekhos Co-Prosperity Sphere. A bit of a pompous title if you ask me. Used to be a splendid king. He saved Mekhos countless times from countless dreadful enemies. But he can't save us now, because this time he's the one trying to *deactivate* us! The king is holding the Robonomicon captive and has decided that we shall all be disassembled."

Code sighed. He was wrong again. There was only one other human here and it was some king, not his grandfather. "The Robo-nob-inon?" asked Code, badly butchering the pronunciation. "Who is that?"

"Are you serious?! The Robo*nom*icon is a sacred relic. It holds the schematics of everyone in Mekhos, our history and the laws that we must operate by. It was created by the original builders. He who controls the Robonomicon controls Mekhos. Of course, the Great Disassembly could change everything."

Disassembly. It was an ominous word. Code thought about taking apart a jigsaw puzzle and stuffing the pieces back in the box. Sensing that he might come to regret the answer, Code was almost afraid to ask the next question: "What do you mean, Great Disassembly?"

"Pow! Kaput. Finished! I'm sorry to be the one to inform you, but all of our warranties are about to be voided! When the Great Disassembly comes, every robot in Mekhos will first be broken down into its component parts. Second, those parts will be broken down into *their* component parts. Third . . . why, there *is* no third. There won't be anybody left. It will be the end of Mekhos. So have a great day, because it's probably your last!"

Just as he'd predicted, Code regretted having asked. Then an uncharacteristically brave idea struck him: "Well, then, why doesn't somebody rescue the Robonomicon and stop the Disassembly?"

The infinipede shook its great head sadly.

"Only a human being can wield the Robonomicon. It was made by the ancient humans to control the experiment that is Mekhos. We robots can't use it. Humans didn't want the inmates running the asylum, understand? No, brute, we are destined for Disassembly."

Clearly, thought Code, *these robots are not very good at spotting human beings.*

"Where is this . . . thing?" he asked.

"You mean the Robonomicon?" replied the infinipede. "It can be found in the Celestial City of His Excellency the— Well, you know the rest. It's very simple, really. Just go directly through the lethal Toparian Wyldes, beyond the endless wastes of the Nanoscopic Traverse, across the uncrossable Fomorian Sea, up the poisonous Mercurial River, to the Right Eyeland; and then straight to the top of the unclimbable Beamstalk."

The infinipede pointed one mandible at a shimmering line rising from the distant horizon. At the top of it, a small light winked. "At the top of that light beam is the Celestial City. It's a hundred thousand miles high, and there are just as many ways to die between here and there. These woods are perfectly safe in comparison."

The infinipede eyed Code. "You look awfully delicate. What is it that you're made of, anyway? Stretchy plastic? I'm surprised you haven't been eaten alive by a cloud of renegade nanospores by now. Listen, little brute. You seem to be completely lost and alone and in terrible danger. Why don't you scamper back to where you came from?"

It was true, thought Code. Peep was gone and he was lost. His curiosity was not worth dying for. *What am I doing? I could get hurt out here, or even killed.* Better to slink back through the Odd Woods and look for the cave and the mound and the school bus. *The safest course of action to take is none at all*, he reminded himself.

Code shrugged and gave a halfhearted wave to the long silver creature. He began to walk into the woods, back the way he had come. As the glade behind him faded into the gloom, he heard the infinipede mutter something to itself in a glum, raspy voice: "If only things could be different. John Lightfall used to be such a *good* king."

Goose bumps spread over Code's shoulders and down his arms.

"What did you say?" he called back to the creature.

The infinipede used its mandibles to briskly wipe splattered bugs and mud away from its compound eyes. It was crouched down, prepared to run away. "John Lightfall, my little brute. He's our king. The one who's going to deactivate our entire world."

It couldn't be a coincidence. Code's grandfather had disappeared near Mek Mound a year ago, and there was a man here with the *same* name?

"John Lightfall is your king?!"

"No more questions, little brute. They are building more of me at the factory all the time. Every second I spend here dillydallying with you causes a backup on the Mainline. I can't stop again or there will be a major catastrophe!"

Code couldn't believe this news. His grandfather? King of the robots? He pushed all thoughts of danger out of his head. *I don't have any choice*, he thought.

"Wait," Code said meekly.

The infinipede blinked at him impatiently.

"Do you mind if I just . . . step under you?"

The infinipede glanced over at its wall of legs. "Very well. But you're signing your own deactivation orders."

Code climbed through the legs of the infinipede to the other side. "Thanks."

"See you at the Disassembly!" called the infinipede.

The creature hunched down and darted away into the underbrush. A split second later, its rear body began to churn forward again, creating a moving silver barrier. Code watched it accelerate into a blur.

It dawned on him that now there really *was* no going back.

Ahead, soaring high above the dark trees, Code saw the Beamstalk stretching up into the sky. At the top of it was the Celestial City, his grandfather and the Robonomicon. *I did it*, thought Code. *Well. I did* something, *anyway*.

A chill wind rolled in from the rapidly darkening woods ahead, and Code shivered. He was on his own in a strange land. Without another moment's hesitation, he took a resolute step forward—towards his destiny, be it great or terrible.

And at that precise moment, Code heard the most wonderful sound he could have imagined: the hum of a tiny pair of robotic wings and a happy chirp. It was Peep! In the shadowed foliage, she sat on a tree limb, glowing a glad shade of gold, watching him. At his approach, she darted towards him and landed on his shoulder, tickling his neck with her fluttering wings.

She was jumping for joy.

Code cupped the tiny robot in both hands and looked down at the softly gleaming creature. Her radiance bathed his face in a warm golden glow. Together, they formed a small island of light in an otherwise shadowy and foreboding forest.

"Did you find me for a reason, Peep?" whispered Code. Her only response was to glow mysteriously. "Either way, I'm glad you came back," he said. "Now let's go and find my grandfather."

3
King John Lightfall

For the next few hours, Code trudged through deep hollows and dark woods. The sun dipped towards the horizon, casting long, still shadows on to the forest floor. Peep buzzed confidently onward without wavering. The little robot never slowed down, although Code's feet were beginning to feel a bit tender.

All at once, a speeding blur rocketed past him and knocked Peep out of the air. She hit the ground hard and peeped in alarm. Before Code could scoop her up, something the size of a saucepan zoomed past his face and crashed into a tree, spraying flecks of metal bark. It looked like a big armoured mechanical beetle. Then a swarm of twinkling, acorn-sized metallic bugs zoomed after it; they landed on the big beetle and began to scrape off bits of bark and mud that were stuck to it.

"What the—?" said Code.

A cacophony of buzzing, flapping and humming ensued as a swarming cloud of mechanical insects of all shapes and sizes came bursting through the forest. Code ducked as a ruby red dragonfly with gear-spun wings droned past his head. Small round bugs sputtered in all directions, pummelling Code in the arms and back like colourful ball bearings. The cloud of insects was in a panic, careening off each other and bouncing off the trees. In the confusion of swirling insects and dust and falling metallic leaves, Code lost sight of Peep.

"Peep! Where are you?"

Code stumbled through the whirlwind, protecting his eyes with one arm and batting away tinfoil flies with the other. At one point, he had to reach into his shirt to pull out a large, purple roly-poly with folded wings that had scampered up his sleeve to hide. Through the noise and confusion Code heard a familiar peeping sound and saw flashes of green light.

"Peep!"

Code bolted towards the bursts of light and into an open glade. Peep was clinging to a tree limb, shooting beams of green light at the other flying insects to keep them away. Code reached out and cradled Peep protectively against his chest. He struggled into the middle of a small clearing.

This world is crazy, thought Code. *How am I ever going to get anywhere?* "What's happening?" he shouted over the vibrating din of beating wings.

Suddenly, the clearing fell silent. The swarm of flying armoured insects slowed and each one dropped to the ground. Their antennae quivered and some of them emitted frightened chirps and squeaks.

The sky was lit by a strange glow.

Code dropped Peep into his shirt pocket, found the tallest tree around and began climbing. The tree limbs were hard as rock and just as sturdy. From his pocket, Peep made a sad, scared warble. But Code was intent on reaching the top. All around, the sky was darkening quickly, as if someone were dimming the lights.

Finally, Code reached the top branches. In the distance, he saw the narrow thread of the Beamstalk climbing straight up into the heavens. Somewhere high up at the top, where the deep blue sky began to fade into the blackness of space, was a speck that he knew was the Celestial City—floating in orbit above the planet and tethered to the surface by a cord of light. The city glinted weakly in the fading sunlight.

Then a ribbon of shimmering colour burst from the Celestial City and projected a large square on to the sky. It was like a movie—big enough for all of Mekhos to see. Numbers appeared, counting down: five, four, three, two, one . . .

The hologram of a giant face appeared: an old man, kindly and round.

"It's my grandpa," whispered Code, elated.

But Code's happiness quickly turned to horror as the man's mouth twisted into a fierce snarl. Black cords wrapped and coiled themselves around the man's neck and head. The coils of wire moved constantly, like snakes. In a voice that was not his grandfather's, the old man croaked: "My good robots, I am John Lightfall, King of the Greater Mekhos Co-Prosperity Sphere and Liege Lord of all its Mechanical Peoples. To the fair bots of Mekhos, I come bearing vile tidings. After a thorough and careful review of the Robonomicon, I have determined that the vast majority of your current programs are outdated, incompatible and—most of all—dangerous. My faithful personal adviser, Immortalis, has instructed me that, in order to fulfill the wishes of the ancient builders, all the robots of Mekhos must *disassemble*."

The view widened, revealing more of the king's body. Code gaped at the grotesque image projected on to the sky like a movie.

The machine called Immortalis looked like a giant black squid. It supported the king's body with thousands of black cords attached to a black oval frame. The tentacles stretched from the machine and wrapped around his body—his arms, legs, torso and even his head and face. Tiny cords wrapped around his fingers and a large solid one encircled his chest. Hundreds more hung limply, swaying in the air. Some cords had nasty-looking suckers and others carried obscure tools. And directly above John Lightfall's head, a milky blue porthole was embedded into the frame of the powerful machine. It looked like a single, unblinking sapphire eye.

The eye of Immortalis blazed as the king continued to

croak: "And so it has been decreed. The great experiment is over. In five days, Mekhos will be returned to its original state. And once you robots are disassembled, the old rifts to the human world will be reopened!"

The king gestured violently at the Beamstalk.

"All robots, automatons and mechanicals are hereby ordered to progress to the heart of Mekhos. To where light meets darkness. To the root of the Beamstalk and the foot of the Celestial City. Make haste! Fly, crawl, or run! By any means necessary—get yourselves to Disassembly Point!"

As Code watched, the swarm of robotic insects began to stir, climbing nearby trees and stretching their wings. One by one, the horde lifted off and began buzzing eastward—towards the Beamstalk. The haze of insects engulfed the treetops and then continued on, away from the amber sunset.

Then a blazing ray of white light shot from Code's shirt pocket and slashed upwards through the sky. Nearly blinded, Code scrambled to grab a branch. For a split second, the beam pierced the golden sky, flashing and pulsing in a complex pattern. It disappeared before Code could see it clearly. Peep glowed hot against Code's chest.

"Peep?" Code asked. "What did you do?"

In the sky, the wasted form of King John Lightfall began to look around. He whispered a single, barely recognisable word: "Code?" Somehow, Peep had alerted the king that he was in Mekhos.

"Grandpa," whispered Code. For an instant, he could see

the kindness return to the eyes of his grandfather. This was the man Code remembered. The quiet man who had led him on long rambling walks through damp woods.

Then the cruel snarl returned to the old man's face. He roared in anger: "A human?! What is a filthy human doing in Mekhos?"

Frightened, Code scrambled down the tree as the voice of the king boomed through the air like distant thunder. His grandfather had seemed intent on destroying every robot in the world. And yet, for one second, Code had seen the kind face that he remembered from before.

It must have something to do with that machine, thought Code. *My grandfather would never act that way. But that black tentacled creature . . . Maybe it's forcing him to say those terrible things. Either way, my real grandfather is here*, Code realised. *And I've got to find him.*

"What have you got us into?" Code whispered to his shirt pocket as he made his way further down the towering tree.

A sleepy, happy chirp came from Peep. Code's pocket glowed a dull gold and vibrated with a contented hum. The exhausted little bot seemed to have fallen asleep and begun to snore. It was a comforting sound. *My only friend is the size of a hummingbird*, thought Code. And it seemed as though she had been just as happy as Code to see John Lightfall.

Finally, Code hopped from a low branch on to solid ground. He patted his pocket and gazed up at the twinkling dot of light that was the Celestial City. His grandfather was alive and maybe in trouble. The Beamstalk was very far away, and this place was unpredictable and frightening. But Code could feel a soothing purr from his shirt pocket. Peep was unafraid. And if such a little creature could be so dedicated and fearless, Code knew that he could, too.

4

Crystalline Castle

The Great Disassembly:
T–Minus Five Days

As the sun began to set, Code and Peep travelled along a wide path of beaten-down grass. She made a pretty handy flashlight, but Code had grown tired and sleepy by the time they rounded a corner to see a ruined castle perched on a gentle hillside. The castle was huge and magnificent and built out of cloudy white blocks of transparent crystal. The walls were overgrown by steel-cable vines, and boulder-sized chunks had crumbled down the hill and rolled away. The doors and windows appeared to be three times as big as usual. *That's curious*, thought Code.

Code ran his fingers over the cool, rough walls of the courtyard. The woods behind him were dark and cold, and the glowing crystalline castle flickered from within, warm and inviting.

Code promised himself he would set out for the Beam-stalk the very next morning, but first he had to find a safe place to sleep for the night. He crept up the path to the castle door, hopping lightly from one massive paving stone to the next. The front door was made of four tree trunks lashed crudely together with thick steel bands. A weathered old robot head protruded from the door, a radar antenna rotating on its head and a large ring clenched in its jaws. Standing on his tiptoes, Code reached up and tried to pull the knocker. It was too heavy to move. So with one shoulder, he shoved against the door with all his might. With a slow squeal, the oversized door opened a crack.

"Hello?" called Code.

No response.

"Peep?" peeped Peep.

Just an echo.

With a final fearful gaze into the dusky courtyard and the shadowy forest beyond, Code slunk through the crack of the door and into the castle.

What he saw inside made him gape in wonder. Everything was giant-sized: a pair of mechanical boots lay near the door, as high as Code's chest; a coat the size of a ship's sail hung on a hook; and a lacy purple umbrella covered in solar panels rested in a barrel-sized pot. Code pinched his nose. The smell wafting out of the enormous black boots was unfathomably stinky, like bad fish and petrol.

The cavernous room was empty and silent—nobody home.

Code wandered through the entrance and down a

hallway until he came to a kitchen, where a bathtub-sized pot of stew was simmering. He dipped a finger into the stew—still warm. As the castle seemed abandoned, Code thought nobody would mind if he just took a little bit. He cupped his palms together and slurped it up. It was like drinking a bucketful of water filled with copper pennies, but it filled his belly. Code smacked his lips and sighed happily. But when he tried to eat a green wafer covered with shiny dots, he nearly chipped a tooth.

Feeling groggy after his feast, Code trudged back to the entrance, climbed the billowing coat and lowered himself into an immense pocket. Inside, he curled up and rested his head on a giant-sized chunk of pocket lint. He smiled, seeing Peep similarly curled up inside his own, much smaller pocket. Safely cocooned, Code fell fast asleep.

The next morning, a tremendous shriek echoed through the castle.

Code's stomach lurched as he was swung violently through the air. Through the fabric of the pocket, he could see morning light filtering through the cloudy walls of the castle.

Someone or something had come home and put on the coat that Code was in.

"Brutus!" shouted a feminine voice. "Something has been eating our circuit board stew!"

A deep voice responded: "It's a filthy mechano-rat, Darla.

You can bet your backup circuits! My osmotic sensors are never wrong!"

Peep peeked out of Code's pocket and buzzed at him in fright.

"I know, I know," whispered Code.

Likewise, Code peeked his own head out. He was in the pocket of a giant robot coat, the owner of which was clanking down a dim hallway in a cloud of wet steam and a racket of pistons.

"I'll find that rat wherever it hides," muttered the huge robot. *This must be the one the other robot called Brutus*, thought Code. *He certainly* sounds *like a brute.*

Code swayed in the air as the monster toddled forward on two primary legs, with several smaller ones hanging awry and occasionally pushing off walls or helping to catch the giant's balance at the last minute. In addition to the coat, the great shabby creature was clothed in a wild confusion of faded robes, capes and frilly smocks. As it moved, it swivelled its small, metal-sheathed head back and forth. Code could feel the throbbing heat from its internal furnace and his ears rang from the awful scraping of its clawed feet against the floor, but there was no opportunity to jump out of the pocket.

"Is the mechano-rat in . . . here?" inquired Brutus, throwing open a massive door. It looked to be some kind of game room. The robot checked each pocket of the billiards table.

A rack of telescoping pool cues bounced up and down nervously, but nothing else moved. Then Brutus checked behind the heat-seeking darts and the soot-covered dartboard. Nothing. Finally, Brutus slammed the door shut and stalked away down the hall.

"What about in . . . here?!"

Brutus yanked open a door to the dining room. He searched behind a pair of chattering, self-shaking salt and pepper shakers. He shooed the four-legged dinner table out of the room and it galloped away with its motors grinding, followed by the chairs. But he found nothing hiding underneath. He tore the metal shutters off the reinforced china cabinet and looked behind the square-, cube-and hypercube-shaped dishes. Again, nothing. Brutus growled in frustration and stomped off towards the next room.

"Maybe Ratty is in . . . here?" Brutus leaped into the kitchen and plunged his long, many-jointed arm into the pot of stew.

"Stop that, you dim bulb!" said the robot with the female-sounding voice. She wore a dress the size of a circus tent and carried a large, splintery broom.

Brutus's small eye visor blinked angrily. "Darla, I am trying to catch a fierce mechano-rat. Lower your volume!"

While the giants argued, Code seized his chance. He carefully climbed out of the pocket, hung over the side and dropped to the floor. Luckily, the giants were so focused on

38

arguing with each other they didn't notice the human boy at their feet. He prayed that the monsters wouldn't catch and eat him, and that no swinging legs would smear him into a boy-coloured paste.

"You couldn't catch a cold— Wait." Darla sniffed loudly. "Brutus, I smell carbon dioxide."

"Carbon dioxide? What could be breathing oxygen?"

"Only one creature breathes oxygen . . . ," murmured Darla.

"King Lightfall *told* us to be on the lookout for . . . ," said Brutus.

Together, both of the gigantic, savage robots bellowed in pure terror.

"*Hoo-mans!*"

"How horrid!"

"Their blood is full of oxygen."

"It's a poison!"

"And a narcotic."

"Not to mention illegal."

Code crept past the giants' primary, secondary and tertiary legs and hid behind a stack of firewood. In a panic, Brutus and Darla shuffled past Code's hiding spot and out of the kitchen. As they lumbered by him, the heat from their engines grew to a furnace blast and the noise of the giant robots' pistons reached an earsplitting roar. Brutus followed Darla out of the door, trailing a stale-smelling cape made of glinting silver scales. The cape rattled along the floor, dragged up against the wall and finally disappeared around the corner.

At last, Peep climbed out of Code's shirt pocket. Very, very quietly, the trembling robot made a relieved *peep!*

The sound echoed through the crystalline castle.

"What what what?" shouted Darla, from the next room.

"Who who who?" shouted Brutus.

"Why why why?" muttered Code.

In an earthquake of movement and a tornado of sound, the two giants stampeded back into the kitchen and, heads swivelling, spotted Code.

"It's . . . it's . . . really a *hoo-man*," shouted Brutus, apoplectic with the horror of his discovery. "Call the king, Darla."

Darla threw one pincered hand over her garishly painted face shield and collapsed in a dead faint, smashing into the nearest wall. Spectacular sconces and moth-eaten portraits of long-rusted robot ancestors collapsed in an avalanche of bad taste. When the rumbling aftershocks had died down, Brutus leaned in to inspect the boy.

Code smiled nervously into Brutus's blazing red eye slit. "Sorry I ate your stew."

Brutus leaped up and covered his mouth grill with a grease-stained handkerchief. "The hoo-man is made of organic matter. How disgusting!"

Having recovered, Darla weakly handed Brutus a broom. "Make it hold still! I'll catch it in a basket!"

"You don't have to do that. I'll just go," offered Code reasonably.

"There's no time, Darla. We'll have to squish it with the broom!" roared Brutus, raising the broom high.

"Excuse me?" asked Code.

"Oh, it's squeaking at us! Smash it quickly! I don't want to look!" mewled Darla.

The broom wavered dangerously back and forth, ready to crush Code at any second.

Code knew that he had to do something immediately or he was a goner. As the broom started to fall, Code racked his brain for something, anything. Suddenly, it came to him.

He threw his arms over his head and twisted his hands into claws.

"*Rawr!*" yelled Code, unconvincingly, he thought.

But the giants froze in place, terrified.

"I *am* a hoo-man! *Rawr!* And I will . . . hurt you with my mighty hoo-man fists!"

Peep hopped on to Code's shoulder and flared her tiny wings. She flashed an angry red as Code stomped towards the giants, waving his arms as though having a fit.

The huge broom dropped to the floor, forgotten. The giants each took a step back, gaping at each other.

"And . . . and I've got *people rabies!*" shouted Code, slobbering and sputtering and frothing furiously at the mouth.

Darla fled immediately. As Brutus turned to watch her go, Code made a dash for freedom. He scampered down the hallway, through the first door he found, and found himself in a vast, cold ballroom. He leaped over gouges and scars left on the floor by the brutal footsteps of generations of dancing robot giants. Finally, Code spotted a crack in the far wall, made a dash and squeezed through it.

This time he was in a room filled with giant-sized books. And on the far wall, beyond an expanse of plush, knee-high carpeting, Code saw a small wooden door. It was human-sized and painted black. To each side of it, a statue of a fierce robot giant stood guard. The surface of the door was intricately carved with an assortment of melting gargoyle-like faces. Some of the creatures seemed to be smiling with laughter, but others were screaming in terror. The whole creepy carving felt as if it were moving just a bit too slowly to see.

Code shuddered. This foreboding door was his only hope.

"What do you suppose the statues are guarding?" Code asked Peep. She just made a small, curious chirp.

All around him, the crystalline castle echoed with the shouts and stomps of rapidly advancing robo-giants as they searched for one very small human being. There was no other choice. Code waded through the carpeting, pushed the ominous, coal black door open and stepped across the threshold.

5

Fabrication Tank

The Great Disassembly:
T—Minus Four Days

Code found himself in a huge cylindrical room. Shafts of sunlight cascaded through a glass dome three stories overhead. Swirling dust motes danced in the empty air. Bookshelves, stocked with thousands of crumbling tomes, stretched upwards, crisscrossed by spindly ladders. A rickety old machine dominated the middle of the room. It looked like a gargantuan microscope aimed at a thick slab of metal resting solidly on the ground.

Peep scurried out of Code's shirt pocket and leaped into the air. She darted from place to place, examining everything with green beams of light. Safe for the moment, Code shoved his hands into his pockets, leaned against the door and exhaled deeply.

Just then a wobbly, wheeled robot creaked out from behind a pile of musty books. Startled, Code yanked his hands out of his pockets, dropping a piece of paper. It was the drawing of the atomic slaughterbot he had made in school. Before he could pick it up, the curmudgeonly robot snatched it away.

In a slow, windy voice it said, "Hmm ... what have we here? The fabrication tank was last activated four hundred and ninety-two years ago. Haven't seen a human in quite some time. But we'd be happy to make this for you, sir."

"Sorry?"

"Hold," said the robot curtly. It adjusted a pair of cracked spectacles on its face and scowled down at the page.

"Can I have that back, please?" asked Code, reaching for the paper.

The robot held up one dismissive clamp. Code stood there frowning, too polite to just snatch the paper away. Peep zoomed past and shot angry beams of red light that the half-blind robot simply brushed away. "Scanning that design for you just now, sir."

Another clawed arm popped up over the robot's shoulder and a beam of blue light shot out. It rapidly traced the contours of the drawing. Wherever the blue light touched the paper, it burst into flame. In a matter of seconds, the page sprinkled to the floor as burning confetti.

"Hey! That was mine!" said Code.

"Very well, sir. We will be delighted to help you. Here in the fabrication tank we like to say that nothing will stand in our way and we will stand in the way of nothing. That includes the creation of your—how do you call it?—atomic slaughterbot."

"What-bot?"

"It really is a strange choice. Probably extremely dangerous, but honestly who am I to judge?"

"Wait," said Code.

"I'm just a simple, lowly clerkbot with a cracked frame and half a battery. I'm in no position to criticise your actions based upon what horrors you may or may not unleash upon yourself, the world and the universe at large through your own blind ignorance, selfishness and/or insanity."

"Just stop for a second," said Code.

"Eh? What I mean to say to you, sir, is this and only this," said the clerkbot, raising one wavering clamper and placing it over Code's mouth to prevent him from speaking. "One atomic slaughterbot, coming up!"

The clerkbot slapped a bell on top of its own head. *Ding!*

Now the huge machine in the middle of the room began to shiver and rumble and wild light sprayed on to the walls. Code fell to the ground, shaken off his feet. The pitted surface of the metal slab began to glow: deep dull red, bright cherry red, orange yellow, yellow white, brilliant white and, finally, dazzling white. Before his eyes, the slab liquefied, forming a white-hot swimming pool of molten metal. Code held on to the wall while the entire smouldering room hummed and thrummed, quaked and quivered. It felt as though the whole castle were about to shake apart.

The giants are sure to hear this, thought Code. Code motioned at Peep to come back, but she ignored him and cavorted merrily through the air. She seemed to be enjoying the mayhem.

Discouragingly, the clerkbot scurried through a small door and slammed it shut. Code heard a *thunk* as the door was locked securely from the other side.

Code flattened himself against the wall as the ponderous microscope machine kept up its crazed activity. Motors whined as the machine whipped back and forth, tracing intricate shapes on to the glowing liquid with pulsing blue lasers. As the lasers etched patterns on to the slab, a shape began to rise up out of the liquid. A menacing form slowly emerged, growing foot by foot into a dark, towering figure.

Finally, it stood motionless and huge in the middle of the room. The machines died down. The lasers stopped. A nozzle sprayed cold swirling clouds of gas on to the slab, cooling down the liquid metal. The room became completely silent and filled with dense mist.

Code heard a low, frightening chuckle boom off the walls. Something was alive on the slab. *This situation has gone from bad to worse*, thought Code. *And now to* worst!

After a few seconds, the mist slowly began to clear.

Stray drops of molten metal rolled across the floor, but the slab was no longer empty. Standing there like an armoured statue was a real version of the atomic slaughterbot from Code's drawing. The thing was over twelve feet tall, with short, awkward legs and long, ape-like arms that hung nearly to the floor. It had a tiny head perched high up on its body. As Code watched, his creation opened its bloodred eye visor and blinked a couple times. It scanned the room and spotted Code.

"Hello, there. I'm Gary, your atomic slaughterbot."

Code was speechless. After a moment, he managed to stammer, "M-my *slaughter*bot?"

"That's right. Of the atomic variety. *Obviously*."

"You . . . slaughter things?"

"You hit the nail on the head, little buddy!"

"Do you do anything else?"

"Afraid not."

"Why . . . slaughter?"

"Well," said the looming slaughterbot, slightly ruffled. "Is a bird happy when it eats a worm? Is a kitten happy when it pounces on a string? Do you blame a wrecking ball for smashing through a building?"

"I suppose not, but—"

"Great. See? I'm designed for slaughtering from the ground up." Gary sighed. "And I do love it so!"

The monstrous robot flexed his battle gauntlets and flipped open a finger cannon thoughtfully. "Oh, slaughter, how I love thee! Let me count the ways!"

And then Gary began to hop around playfully. His reckless dance shook the room and shattered the domed windows above, sending shards of glass raining down. The glass bounced harmlessly from Gary's thick armour, but Code had to throw himself out of the way to avoid it.

Then the hulking robot burst into song:

> Crashing, smashing, blasting, wrecking,
> These are the things I love to do!
> Lasering, Tasering, masering, phasering,
> Slaughter, mayhem, I love you!
>
> For I am a slaughterbot,
> I never have to say "Please."
> Even if I am caught,
> I can crush your head with ease.
>
> My principle of attack?
> Leap ahead, never look back.
> My principle of defence?
> I haven't got one—I'm too immense!
>
> My head is extra tiny,
> My arms are extra large,
> My lasers extra shiny,
> And I keep 'em fully charged.
>
> My motors roar, my huge arms bend,
> That crashing sound, it is your end.
> Turn around, and run away,
> For I'm about to slaughter—yay!

Gary stopped dancing and looked around at the devastated room. Code swallowed, certain he was about to be flattened. Peep chirped, annoyed by the dust and destruction.

"It's just a little song I wrote about slaughtering," Gary said modestly.

There was nowhere to run. Code was trapped in this room with a chatty, oversized slaughterbot. And the only way to survive seemed to be to . . . talk to it.

"That's really, uh, nice," Code called up to Gary. "But can't you do something *besides* slaughter?"

Gary thought for a microsecond. "No. That doesn't make any sense. I'm a slaughterbot, plain and simple. In fact, I better get on with the slaughtering! You'll excuse me if I unscrew your head from your body now?"

Gary reached for Code with a crane-like arm. *This is it,* thought Code. *My head is about to be crushed into jelly.* Code squeezed his eyes shut as the metal hand loomed closer and closer. And then he abruptly remembered something that Gary had said.

"Wait. You're *my* atomic slaughterbot?"

Gary paused. "That's right. And who are you?"

"I'm Code, and I need to ask you for a favour."

"Anything for you, Code." Gary waited for Code's command.

Code took a deep breath and then blurted it out: "No slaughter."

"Come again?"

"No slaughtering. You can't slaughter."

"Once more?"

"You aren't allowed to slaughter anyone. No slaughtering. Can't slaughter. No. Slaughter."

"Not quite sure I understand. Are you saying that I should *not* slaughter? Or is this a metaphor? Or some sort of riddle? I'm not very good at riddles. Only slaughtering."

Just then a thunderous knock sounded on the other side of the door. Code heard the booming voice of Brutus, bellowing angrily.

"Gary," urged Code, "we've got to escape from here! Can you bash a hole in the wall?"

"Can't."

"Why?"

"I'm not allowed to slaughter."

Code pointed at a wall of old books and ladders and papers. "Gary! Slaughter that wall!"

Gary hopped up and down and clapped his metal-sheathed hands together.

"You got it!" With a gleeful giggle, Gary raised both fists high in the air and smashed through the wall, sending stones, chunks of crystal and shards of glass erupting into the courtyard. Without looking back, Gary lumbered through the gaping hole, chuckling happily. With much less enthusiasm, Code and Peep climbed through the hole and onward to freedom.

6

Grassy Glade

The Great Disassembly:
T–Minus Four Days

"Be honest. Are you going to slaughter me?" asked Code.

With Brutus and Darla in close pursuit, Code and Gary had hurried through the countryside and away from the crystalline castle. Eventually, the booms of the robot giants firing their guns had died away. The mechanical woofs of hunting quadrupeds had also trailed off. Now that they had stopped running and begun to walk, Code felt it was time to ask the question.

"Nope," said Gary in a matter-of-fact tone.

"Good, because you aren't allowed to," said Code.

Gary's word was good enough for Code. It would have to be, since he couldn't outrun Gary even if he tried. Also, Peep seemed to be happy. She flickered ahead through the tall grass, always on a beeline for the Beamstalk that stretched like a thread on the horizon. *Who knows*, thought Code. *An atomic slaughterbot might make a good ally.*

"So, if you're a human, who is the little one?" asked Gary.

"I call her Peep," said Code. And then, just to be sure, he added, "And she's off-limits, too."

"You got it," replied Gary.

Peep flew up and landed on Gary's shoulder. She trundled around in little circles, inspecting him. Gary managed to crane his neck and focus on her.

"Where did you find her?"

"In my world. She led me here."

"She is very small. You should protect her."

"I will," said Code solemnly.

The lumbering robot and small boy walked together into the dusk, through metallic blades of grass and over rolling hills. The journey reminded Code of the hikes he and his grandfather used to take through the woods back home— just the sound of footsteps, the feel of sweat evaporating from his forehead, the smell of the woods.

As they walked, they talked.

"Gary?"

"Yeah, Code?"

"Where did you come from?"

"From the fabrication tank."

"But how?"

"From your schematics."

"That was just a drawing I made up."

"It must have been a pretty great drawing, if I do say so myself. You're an excellent artist, for a human." Gary flexed his arm pistons and chuckled. Then, in a more serious tone, he added, "Imagination is valuable, Code. The trick is to turn it into reality."

The tinny sound of crickets permeated the dense grass. Code followed the *screep, screep* sound to a thicket. He pulled a patch of grass aside, but found only a small green speaker. It broadcast the cricket noise over and over again.

This place is totally unpredictable, thought Code. *I need all the help I can get.*

As they marched onward, Code wondered aloud, "Gary? Why are you coming with Peep and me?"

"Well, Code, I don't want to sound mean, but you and Peep seem very . . . flimsy. And you aren't very big at all. Since I've got to be disassembled anyway, I might as well help you follow the great exodus to Disassembly Point. King's orders, you know. Even a newborn robot like me is programmed to know that much."

"Why would the king order that?" asked Code. "Won't he be disassembled like everyone else?"

"Nope," replied Gary. "Only robots can be disassembled. The king and his adviser will survive. Which is too bad for you humans. Once the experiment of Mekhos is over, the rifts will open. Immortalis will be able to go to your world. And it doesn't seem like a very nice robot. All those . . . *tentacles.*"

Gary shivered.

"Oh, no," muttered Code. "Why would Immortalis want to go to Earth?"

"I hope you don't have to find out, Code," replied Gary. "But the rifts to your world won't open until there are no more robots left in Mekhos. They're built that way to protect the human world from us. Immortalis can't leave until after the Disassembly, and it can't leave without the human king."

Code could only imagine that murderous monster bursting out of Mek Mound and attacking people with its razorsharp tentacles. Who knew what kind of mayhem Immortalis would cause in the real world?

"*You're* not really going to be disassembled, though, are you?" asked Code, a little afraid.

Gary's only response was to shrug and say, "I'm a robot. Deactivation is just another part of programming."

Code looked at his thin arms and clenched his fists. For the first time ever, he had friends. Sure, they were robots. One of them was the size of a grasshopper and the other was big as a house. *They're weird*, he thought. *But then again, so am I.*

It didn't matter. They were his friends.

Code patted the massive slaughterbot on one plate-covered leg. "Don't worry, Gary. I'm going to find the Robonomicon and save Mekhos."

"Thanks, Code. I *was* only created this morning. I'm too young to be disassembled."

Code chuckled. "You seem pretty mature for a robot who was just made," he said.

"I'm not just *any* robot. I'm an atomic slaughterbot model number nine-oh-two. Randomly selected individual name for smooth human interactions: Gary."

"But you already know how to walk and talk. That took me years to learn."

"Walking and talking come standard as part of the Tome of Knowledge of the Well-Adjusted Robot. It's the basic education that every Mekhosian slaughterbot comes equipped with."

"You're lucky. I have to go to school," said Code.

"Oh," said Gary. "I did a brief stint."

"When? I've been with you since you were born."

"After I landed on the fabrication pad. There was a second or two where I had to move around my arms and legs to figure out how long they were and where my elbows and knees were and how everything worked. Sure, I had a basic idea of how to do it from the Tome. But the rest I just sort of picked up along the way."

Gary looked at his stubby finger cannons, then wiped them on his chest modestly. "Why? How long does school take? Ten microseconds? Twenty?"

"Uh. About twelve years to finish high school. Another four years for college. Another two or four or six if you want to be a doctor or lawyer or scientist."

Gary shuddered in horror. "Twenty *years* of school?" He burst into laughter, startling a nest of robo-starlings into flight.

"It does seem silly," said Code, thinking about how nice it would be to finish school in a couple of seconds. "But it can be sort of fun, sometimes," he added, thinking of Hazel.

The sun was beginning to set on the meadow they were walking through. All around them, small, brightly coloured light-emitting doodlebugs (LEDs) hopped in tight spirals, leaving light streaks on Code's vision. Peep flitted through the air with the LEDs, flashing her own lights and showing off.

In the distance behind the happy confusion of swooping lights, the deep woods lurked, dark and deadly.

"I'm glad you're here, Gary. We've got a dangerous road ahead of us," said Code.

Gary froze. Abruptly, his right arm broke in half and a cannon slid out and locked into place. The gun cocked and a warbling hum of electricity began to build.

"Where?" whispered Gary.

"Where is what?"

"The dangerous road?"

Code smacked Gary on the leg. "Ahead of us in *time*, Gary! Not in front of us right now!"

"Ahead?" asked Gary, scanning the path with his cannon.

"We've got a dangerous road in the *future*," replied Code.

Gary retracted his cannon and relaxed. "Why'd you say 'ahead,' then?"

Code scratched his head. "It's just how humans talk. When something is going to happen in the future, we say it's 'ahead' of us. And when something already happened in the past, we say that it's 'behind' us. It's kind of weird, now that I think about it."

Gary reached down and lightly cupped the top of Code's head. He turned it from side to side, inspecting it carefully. "I've got it. Most of your sensory organs are located right here in your head area. Your eyes and ears and that other thing in the middle of your face."

"My nose."

"Right. Your eyes, ears and nose are all pointing the same direction—forward."

"So what?"

"That must be why you humans think the future is ahead and the past is behind. Because you go through life always following your eyes and ears and noses."

Code thought about it. "And robots don't?"

Gary's chest swelled with pride. As he spoke, he began to practise little karate chops in the air, positioning himself defensively in front of the tall grass. "Not really. I've got sensors pointed in every direction at once. I can access satellites floating in space. My range finders are pointed front and back. Maybe something's sneaking up from behind?"

Gary jumped and spun around, midair. He swung a hefty paw and scissored a clump of grass in half with one serrated forearm. "*Pow!* Slaughterised!"

Code sneezed and brushed several blades of grass off his shoulders. "That's nice, Gary. You're really remarkable, you know?"

Gary's red eye visor pulsed with sudden emotion. He stopped walking and looked down at Code. In the setting sun, Gary looked to Code like a hazy building looming overhead. Light-emitting doodlebugs danced around them in the twilight and the metallic grass tinkled gently in the evening breeze.

"Thank you, Code," said Gary. "That means a lot."

7

Robot Heroes and Criminals

After walking in the dark for several hours, Code and Gary set up camp beneath a grove of eerily quiet trees. Ever the helper, Gary laser-ignited an emergency flare to create an instant campfire. During the long evening, the two sat leaning against logs with their hands behind their heads. Peep settled down on Code's knee to clean herself. A few moments of comfortable silence passed.

Then, with the firelight dancing in his visor, Gary cleared his throat and began to tell a story. He said that it was his favourite story of all time and that it was about the biggest robot hero—and criminal—who had ever lived in the land of Mekhos:

"Once upon a time, in the dirtiest, darkest factory of the Drudge-Bottom Slums, lived Charlie, a robot worker of the lowest order. Charlie toiled nonstop for shifts that lasted a thousand years. After each shift, the workers were allowed to emerge from the depths of the factory for a one-hour break and a rapid solar recharge. Charlie's job was to paint yellow happy faces on to pieces of cardboard, clothes, or anything else that happened to pass by on the assembly line.

"Because Charlie had such a simple job, he was designed to be a simple robot. All Charlie ever thought about—all that he *could* think about—was painting bright yellow happy faces. You see, Charlie loved making happy faces just like I love slaught—"

Code groaned. "I know! I know! Slaughtering!"

Gary harrumphed and then continued. "But the other robots laughed behind Charlie's back. They would turn his happy faces upside down and, thinking that they had become sad faces, Charlie would spend all day redoing them—only to have them turned upside down again. Charlie was too simpleminded to understand that jokes were being played on him. So when the other robots played mean pranks, he laughed, too. He thought they were his friends. And that only made the mean-spirited robots laugh even harder. Sometimes they would even congratulate each other on being so very smart."

"I hate jerks like that," blurted Code, thinking of Tyler. It seemed that no matter where you went, there was always someone who was trying to make fun of someone else.

Gary shook his head ruefully. "But one day, the jokes went too far. The factorybots took Charlie out to a trash rocket. It was about to be launched on a one-way trip into the Trash Quadrant. They told Charlie that the rocket needed a smiley face on the very top. So Charlie climbed atop the rocket and began painting a happy face on the nose cone. Just then, the rocket ignited. Charlie frantically tried to climb off, but it was too late. The rocket launched with Charlie on board and disappeared into space on a thousand-year journey to nowhere."

Peep chirped sadly and flickered to blue.

"Poor Charlie," said Code.

Gary continued. "After the next thousand-year work shift, the factorybots weren't laughing. News reports had begun to trickle in about strange happenings in deep space. Mysterious radio transmissions had begun to arrive from the Trash Quadrant. It was puzzling since the factorybots had no idea who—if anyone—actually *lived* in the Trash Quadrant. No one had ever bothered to check.

"The factorybots went back to work, but by their next break, the news had become downright terrifying. An unidentified energy pulse had been detected roaring towards Mekhos at an incredible speed. Stars were winking out of the sky in the Trash Quadrant. New planets were disappearing from solar systems closer and closer to Mekhos. Something terrible was coming. King John Lightfall organised the Light Reconnaissance Space Cavalry and reinstated the long-defunct Exo-Spheric Battle Savants; he armed them for combat with the most powerful weapons captured during the Xeno Wars."

"Wow," murmured Code.

"The cruel factorybots knew something disastrous was about to happen," said Gary. "They peered into the sky and shook with dread. They held on to each other and cried out in fright. Then they tried to run away, but there was nowhere to go."

At this point, even little Peep was engrossed in the story. She had stopped cleaning herself midstroke and now stared intently up at Gary. One of her wings was still cocked at a wild angle behind her leg.

After a dramatic pause, Gary said, "In the sky above, looking down with a horrible smile, was a happy face made entirely of displaced stars. Each eye contained a thousand burning orbs, the mouth a hundred thousand more, and surrounding the entire monstrous apparition was the yellowish vapour of a billion shattered solar systems."

Gary smiled and leaned over the campfire. Code took a deep breath. This was clearly Gary's favourite part of the story.

"See, Charlie had been hard at work in deep space. As the workers looked on in horror, a familiar-looking rocket crash-landed next to the launchpad. The rocket was bright yellow, with happy faces painted across every visible surface. Each bolt that held the rocket together had a happy face painted on it. The nose had a happy face. Even the happy faces were made up of happy faces.

"The door opened and little Charlie rolled out, looking the same as ever. He waved to his dear 'friends' and began to paint a happy face on the ground. In the sky, streaks of flame appeared in the atmosphere. Then thousands of atmospheric entry pods roared into view, rapid-launching parachutes carrying hundreds of thousands of identical Charlies—each with a paintbrush and a passion for drawing happy faces. Mekhos was overwhelmed in minutes."

Gary stretched his long arms, joints creaking like an old swing set.

"Charlie's invasion started the Great Garbage Wars, which lasted over a century. Eventually, King John Lightfall and his Exo-Spheric Battle Savants tracked down the original Charlie."

"Wait," interrupted Code. "My grandpa has only been gone for a year. How did he spend a hundred years fighting a crazy robot?"

"Mekhos is an experimental world," replied Gary. "Time goes faster here. The ancient ones set up the experiment so that a hundred years of our time was only a hundred days in their time."

Gary continued. "In the final hours of the final battle, King Lightfall captured Charlie and trapped him inside a stasis box. Mekhos was saved—"

"I knew my grandpa was a good guy," said Code.

Gary shook his head. "But not before Charlie was able to strike one last time. Before King Lightfall could close the box, Charlie used an alien weapon to resculpt the continent of

Mekhos into the shape of an enormous, eternally grinning . . . happy face."

Gary chuckled in the firelight. Peep tittered, amused. Code sat silently, soaking up the story.

"So let me get this straight," said Code. "Charlie nearly destroyed Mekhos. He blasted your continent into the shape of a happy face. He blew up thousands of robots."

"Yeah," said Gary. "He's my hero!"

"How, exactly, does that make him a hero?" asked Code.

"Charlie did what he was programmed to do, completely and without hesitation," replied Gary. "He showed that you don't have to be big to do big things. Charlie made a lot out of a little!"

Peep agreed, violently nodding her tiny head up and down. Gary laughed and threw another flare on the fire. For his part, Code watched his two new friends closely, shaking his head in puzzled amazement.

8

Toparian Wyldes

The Great Disassembly:
T–Minus Three Days

The next morning, sunlight filtered through the trees and Code opened his eyes to find every shade of green imaginable. Looking around, he realised that in the dark of night they had set up camp in a beautiful garden that seemed to go on for miles. The plants here seemed almost real. Gently waving bushes formed vivid green walls. Prickly bridges made of tightly packed shrubs crossed overhead in twisting spirals. Moss-covered statues of robots, machines and animals dotted the gardenscape. Even the grass was tight-growing and spongy, like a trampoline.

Everything smelled like wet grass and mud and metal.

Code smiled to himself. Finally, a nice quiet place without any heart-stopping danger. Then he noticed Gary standing nearby, peeking over a towering bush.

"Good morning, Gary," said Code, yawning.

Gary thunderously dropped to all fours and peered into

Code's face. He rubbed his shiny head with one hand and muttered to himself in a panic. "Oh, Code! Thank goodness you've come back to life. I was sure that you were deactivated. I almost buried you!"

And indeed, Code noticed that he was lying next to a hole about the size of a boy. "I was *sleeping*, Gary," said Code, warily eyeing the freshly dug grave. "Humans go to sleep every day and stay asleep for about eight hours."

"What? You're telling me that humans fall on the ground and go completely limp and unconscious and helpless for eight solid hours every single day? But why? That's just silly!"

"It's true, though."

Climbing out from Code's pocket, Peep chirped fearfully.

Gary continued breathlessly: "You can make up lies about humans later. This is an emergency. Look around. Can't you see we are in serious trouble? We're all about to be killed instantly! Any minute!"

Code sighed and lay back down, looking up at the leafy green foliage. Of course trouble was coming. How long could he expect to actually calm down and enjoy visiting an experimental world designed by a lost civilisation?

"What's the danger, Gary?"

Gary craned his head around nervously. "Last night while we were walking in the dark, we accidentally set up camp in the Toparian Wyldes."

"So?" Code yawned.

"So?! The Toparians are a race of robots designed to trim, sculpt and cultivate greenery. They've been spreading further into the Odd Woods every year. Nobody can stop them!"

"That's why this place is so beautiful," mused Code. He imagined thousands of friendly gardeners, relentlessly pruning every branch, sweeping up every twig and watering every last delicate flower. It was a job too big for any human being. Funny that robots had created a place that looked more natural and beautiful than anything Code had ever seen on Earth.

"They're killers!" shouted Gary, making Code wince. "They don't just trim the woods. *Anything* that enters the Wyldes goes into the equation, if you know what I mean. I don't want to be mowed to death, Code. I'm just a newborn. How are we ever going to escape from the trimmers, hedgers, cutters, snippers, shearers, twiners, shapers, fringers, choppers, loppers, pruners, nippers, thinners, thickerers, cubers, hackers, sawers, gnawers, slicers and dicers?" (To protect Code's emotions, Gary considerately chose not to mention the mulchers, gulchers, composters, sod slingers, bark blasters and ditch rippers.)

Looking closely, Code noticed bits of glinting metal wrapped into the shrubbery, providing architectural support. To his dismay, he realised that the mangled skeletons of long-deactivated robots were mingled in with nearly every plant, lending them all a strange metallic shimmer. A nearby statue was really the rusted corpse of some kind of robot knight. Even the flagstones underfoot seemed to be made out of the shattered remains of robot body parts.

The garden was completely still and quiet, except for Gary's panicked muttering. Peep hopped into the air and hovered low over the ground. She probed the garden with inquisitive green light beams. Then, with a purposeful burst of speed, she took off along a path.

Code stood up and dusted shards of metallic dirt from his trousers. The great shining mass of greenery suddenly made him feel claustrophobic. Green filled his vision, towering above and creeping below. The distant call of a bird took on a sinister note. The creaking of branches sounded ominous. What horrible monsters could be lurking in the depths of this lush paradise?

"It's OK, Gary. Peep will lead us out of here," said Code, pretending to be brave. "Let's get moving."

Following Peep, Code led his lumbering friend steadily through the magnificent gardens. Certain death failed to appear.

A few minutes later, Code felt a tap on his shoulder.

"Code?" whispered the hulking slaughterbot.

"Yes?"

"I'm scared."

To distract Gary, Code pointed to a particularly impressive shrub; it had been pruned into something resembling an elephant with long, thin legs and twin towering topiary tusks. It was at least a hundred feet tall.

"What's that supposed to be?" he asked.

Gary examined the sculpture. "It's a stilt-walker, the royal war steed of Lightfall's Shatter-Gun Brigades. You don't want to be around when one of them shows up. Unless you've got me to protect you, of course."

"Of course," said Code, carefully stepping around one outstretched hoof. Lightfall. Royal. Code wondered again how his grandfather, just an ordinary old man back home, had come to be royalty here in Mekhos. Then again, any human being who could stay alive in this place for a *week* had to be amazing.

As they walked, Code allowed himself to imagine what the Robonomicon would look like—probably a massive golden book with words written in shimmering light. Like a book of magic spells. Code couldn't *wait* to find it.

They pursued Peep and soon found themselves in a clearing with tall, waving grass. It was home to a group of odd trees covered with what looked like glowing lightbulbs. Their smooth, thick branches were pruned completely bare except for puffy tufts of leaves. Planted in a row, the trees looked like a line of trimmed poodles at a dog show.

Gary screeched like a broken can opener and pointed with one trembling finger cannon at the meadow. "Oh, no, Code. The grass." He quaked. "It isn't *mowed!*"

"Gor goodness' sake," said Code, peering through the tall weeds. "Just relax—"

Suddenly, a loud buzzing sound rang through the clearing. Peep flickered past, glowing a scared violet as she darted over the grass and towards the puffy trees. Gary squealed as a flurry of freshly cut grass shot up into the air nearby. The flying grass erupted in a zigzag pattern that raced across the field. Whatever was hidden in the grass was coming towards them—fast.

"Mowers!" shrieked Gary, stomping his huge feet in hysterical fright. (In fact, his body was doing what it does when the brain shouts at it to do *something*, but doesn't tell it what.)

From the corner of his eye, Code saw a bright streak of light as Peep careened away. Thinking quickly, Code grabbed Gary by the finger and pulled him headlong through the grass. The buzzing noise seemed to be coming from every direction. Code and Gary couldn't see anything as they stumbled forward, ribbons of grass and acrid smoke flying everywhere. Finally, Code spotted the trunk of a tree. Just as a mower lurched out of the grass, the boy and the robot leaped for one of the lower branches. It bent alarmingly under their added weight, but held steady. Peep was already waiting on a higher branch, preening nonchalantly.

Below, the monstrous predators were hidden somewhere in the tall grass. The mowers buzzed angrily and circled the tree like sharks, sending plumes of shredded grass into the air. Safe for the moment, Code and Gary perched on the creaking branches and stared morosely at the grass. There was nowhere left to go—they were trapped in a tree in the Toparian Wyldes.

After a few moments, however, all the grass lay in a jumble on the ground. And Code saw the mowers for the first time.

There were two of them. Each was about the size of a dinner table and covered in a thick mat of sod and leaves. They had small heads with tiny, dim eyes that peeked out from under their grassy shells. With all the grass gone, the roar of the mowers' whirling tummy blades had grown quiet. Without the smoke and confusion and cutting, the mowers actually looked a bit like a couple of oversized puppies. Of course, thought Code, when a puppy jumps on your leg, it doesn't chop up your trousers with whirling metal stomach blades.

The boy and the slaughterbot sat in the tree for a long time, trying in vain to come up with a plan to escape. An expert tree climber, Code made his way to the upper branches and found one of the lightbulb-shaped fruits. It glowed and pulsed with a rainbow swirl of delicious-looking colours. But when Code tried to pull it from the branch, the fruit wouldn't budge. Instead, he heard a beeping and booping noise coming from inside the tree. Very faintly, almost lower than the sighing of the wind, Code heard the word "human" being repeated. Suddenly, all the fruit on the trees snapped to a single colour: bright apple red. Code tugged again, and the nearest apple-thing snapped off the tree. It flickered in his hand, and its red light went out. Code took a hesitant nibble. The fruit tasted delicious—like a warm caramel apple with vanilla ice cream in the middle—but it was hard as a rock.

From the ground came a pitiful whine. Looking down, Code saw a mower staring greedily at the lightbulb fruit. It waggled its broad, grassy backside and yapped at him. With a shrug, Code tossed down the apple. The eager mower jumped on to the fruit and devoured it. Afterwards, it barked happily up at Code.

"What just happened?" asked Code.

"You set the tree to human. And the mowers must love people food," said Gary.

That gave Code an idea.

Ten minutes later, Code had collected over a hundred apples and Gary had shoved them all into his chest cavity. Code had explained his plan, but Gary was reluctant. "Don't take your eyes off that mower for two blinks, Code. These woodland Toparians are mighty flighty!"

Hanging by one arm from a low branch, Code held out a fresh fruit to the enthusiastic mowers. One of them bounced forward and knocked its fellow aside to gobble up the fruit. At that moment, Code dropped lightly down on to the mower's back. He wrapped his fingers in the cool grass and vines. The bulky mower didn't even notice. With a small whimper of fright, Gary hopped out of the tree and carefully settled himself on the back of the other mower. The heavily armoured machines ignored them, searching for more food.

"Go!" shouted Code.

Peep chirped happily and pinched herself tightly to Code's forearm. Gary took an apple out of his chest and pitched it like a baseball, rocketing it a hundred yards through the sculpted garden. The mowers sprinted forward eagerly with Code and Gary and Peep hanging on for dear life.

"To the Beamstalk!" Code laughed, unaware that a thousand miles of certain death lay just ahead.

9

Nanoscopic Traverse

The Great Disassembly:
T–Minus Three Days

After riding, napping and playing "I Spy" on the grass-covered backs of the mowers for hundreds of miles, two things happened: Gary ran out of fruit, and the forest gave way to a stark expanse of empty desert. Without any apples to eat, the mowers stopped moving and would venture no further. Luckily, after sharing countless hours (and apples) together, the mowers had become positively friendly towards them. Giving them a pat on their snouts, Gary and Code bade the two loyal beasts farewell. The mowers snuffled off, making their way towards Disassembly Point.

Code watched sadly as the two mowers pounced after each other like mossy puppies. He was going to miss those funny little guys. *Appearances really can be deceiving*, he thought. Then something flickered in the corner of his vision.

Code shaded his eyes and scanned the desert but saw nothing. Shimmering waves of heat blasted off its surface.

In the distance, the Beamstalk glimmered in the sky like an illusion. Peep swooped on top of Code's head, gazed for a moment at the desert, then dropped into the shade of his shirt pocket and fell promptly asleep.

"How are we going to reach the Beamstalk? It must still be a thousand miles away," said Code.

"Eight hundred and forty-three, actually," replied Gary.

"So what are we going to do?"

"Walk," said Gary. "And walk some more."

"Great," said Code.

Code had just taken one small step on to the sand when Gary screeched in fright. "You can't walk *there*!" he exclaimed.

"Why not?" asked Code.

"That's the Nanoscopic Traverse! It's certain death to set foot inside the Traverse."

Code gingerly removed his foot. "But it's just a lot of sand."

"It *looks* like sand. But it's really the remains of cremated robots. The nanobots of the Traverse are too small to see, but there are billions of them. They can swarm over your whole body and dissolve it into sand—just like that."

And Gary snapped his finger cannons—*ping!*

"Oh, no," groaned Code. "What do we have to do, walk all the way around?"

"Affirmative."

"How long will that take?"

"At your maximum walking speed it shouldn't take more than a year, plus or minus an hour."

"But that's too long...," said Code. He could see the Beamstalk gently wavering on the horizon. "We've only got a few days left before the robots are disassembled." Code had a thought. "How are all the other robots going to make it there in time? Can't we go with them?"

Gary looked embarrassed.

"What?" asked Code.

Gary pointed to the sky with one finger cannon. Up above, Code noticed a pattern of very faint dots. The tiny grey specks were slowly moving across the sky towards the Beamstalk.

"Are those robots?" asked Code.

"Yep," said Gary. "They're using the robo-cannons. Mek mortars. Bot blasters. Those big guns can launch a bot across the continent in about five minutes. I hear it's pretty relaxing. One big thump and then smooth sailing. Of course, if *you* tried it, your bones would turn to liquid and your eyeballs would shoot out of your ears."

Code growled in frustration. This was maddening. The robots could just step into a cannon and be launched to their destination in seconds. Meanwhile, he had to fight for every inch.

"Don't feel bad, Code," said Gary. "It's not your fault you're just a delicate human."

Code looked from the skies to the forbidding sand. *Nothing is ever as it seems here,* he reminded himself. Maybe I should stop being surprised when things *aren't* what they seem to be and start being surprised when they *are*. Looking hopelessly out at the flat expanse of sand, Code realised that something was out of place. Surprisingly, he wasn't very surprised.

"What's that?" asked Code, pointing.

A plate-shaped craft floated over the heat-blasted desert floor. The flat platform was covered with robots and tents and rugs. In the centre, a big chair loomed over the tents. The craft rotated slowly as it hovered over the sand.

"Look!" cried Code, rapping on Gary's leg.

"Gary, get their attention," he said. "Those robots can give us a ride across the Traverse."

"I don't know . . ."

"Hurry up!" urged Code. "We're losing them!"

The ship was moving further away.

Reluctantly, Gary aimed a finger straight up. His finger-tip hinged open and a finger cannon belched a ball of flame high into the air. The strange ship instantly changed course, zipping towards them over the sand.

"See, Gary?" said Code. "They're coming to help us already. It looks like they're having a party."

"I don't think so," Gary said.

Code squinted at the ship. As it grew closer, his hope faded. The big chair was a silver throne. And just above it was a familiar form. Immortalis hovered there, tentacles clutching the body of John Lightfall. The party guests were really robot prisoners, chained to each other. Solid-looking robot guards stood in a semicircle around the throne, holding banners that snapped in the hot wind. Suddenly, one of Immortalis's long tentacles snaked out and snatched up a prisoner. It tossed the poor fellow overboard.

"Oh, no!" cried Gary.

The little bot fell from the platform and landed in the desert below. In a panic, it stood up and tried to wheel away. But before it could crawl even a few feet, it began to disintegrate as the nano-sized creatures consumed it. Within seconds, the prisoner dissolved into a puff of sand that blew away in the breeze.

"They're getting rid of prisoners," said Gary. "And now they've seen us."

"C'mon, we've got to hide," said Code, his heart pounding in his chest. In real life, Immortalis was frightening and huge—even from a distance.

Gary and Code turned and fled back towards the trees, away from the desert, until Code was out of breath. With Immortalis safety behind him, Code stopped to take in his surroundings. He heard a whooshing, crashing noise coming from deeper in the woods. Cautiously, he made his way towards the sound and, peering through the trees, he saw a big, flat square of concrete in the middle of a meadow.

Curious, Code marched over to the slab and stood on top of it.

"What is this?" he asked Gary, who followed close behind.

"Certain death!" boomed Gary.

Code sighed angrily. "Why is everything always certain death with you?"

"Code red! Relocate immediately!" shouted Gary.

A sudden rush of wind blew past and tree limbs began to crash down around them. Code stumbled away from the square slab of concrete just as a crab-like creature plummeted down through the forest canopy. With six brawny legs extended, it landed on the slab with a bone-jarring thud. Finally, the whole nimble machine settled down onto its flexible hind legs, then turned in place.

"Where did that come from?" asked Code.

"It's a transped," answered Gary. "They travel across Mekhos by hopping from one slab to another. I doubt this is its final destination."

It was true. With a playful wiggle, the machine suddenly unleashed all the pent-up force in its muscular robotic legs and shot into the sky over the Nanoscopic Traverse. In its wake, a flurry of leaves and branches fell to the ground. A stray tree limb smashed down with unnatural force and shattered into tiny metal flecks. Code jumped out of the way, narrowly avoiding having his brain mashed into pink goo.

Then the shimmering flecks of metal from the shattered limb melted, forming a shallow river that flowed like syrup towards the desert sands.

"What the heck?" said Code.

"A nanotree," said Gary. "Built out of a whole colony of

nanobots invading from the Traverse. Pretty common here on the fringes."

Code looked at Gary, puzzled.

Gary explained further. "Billions of tiny robots from the desert have got inside the tree and turned it into a big chunk of metal. That's why it weighs as much as a boulder. You're lucky you weren't squished."

"Squished by nanobots too small to see?"

"Yeah." Gary chuckled. "How embarrassing would that be?"

By now, the nanobots from the various broken limbs had spread out and joined together into inky black pools of liquid. The pools were creeping over the ground and forming into a larger pool—one that was encircling them both.

"Cheese and crackers," muttered Gary.

Peep popped out of Code's shirt pocket and scurried down the length of his arm, tickling him as she probed the pool of liquid with green beams of light. Then she skittered up Code's arm and perched on his shoulder, glowing red and defiant.

"Why is it surrounding us, Gary?" asked Code. "Are these things dangerous?"

The two broad ends of the pool met and combined, creating a ring of thick black liquid that completely surrounded them. A menacing ripple went through the liquid.

"Only if they're hungry," said Gary.

"Are they hungry?"

Gary didn't reply.

"Are they hungry, Gary?" Code repeated.

The pool closed in tighter.

"I'm afraid they're always hungry, Code."

"Right," groaned Code. He was getting very tired of running away from menacing robots, large and small.

"Maybe we can jump—," said Code, but was interrupted by a sharp *crack!*

Just then, an entire tree crashed down and exploded into a flood of inky sludge. The circling pool of nanobots was forgotten as Code spotted the nose of the plate-shaped desert craft. It had found them and was pushing its way into the woods, breaking huge trees in half. Hovering above the silver throne, Immortalis gave commands to its stone-faced robot guards. All the prisoners were gone, presumably thrown into the desert. As the craft shoved its way into the clearing, the blue eye of Immortalis glared at them hatefully. It was then that Code noticed his grandfather hanging limply from Immortalis's black tentacles.

"Stop, human!" shouted his grandfather. Only it *wasn't* his grandfather, Code had to remind himself. He swallowed a pang of sadness at the sight of that familiar face twisted into an angry snarl. Code wished he could hear his grandfather's true voice just for a moment, but John Lightfall was under the control of that horrible monster.

Peep chirped, fluttered her wings and shot a beam of light back at the landing pad. Code backed up to the edge of the nanobot sludge. Gary stood beside the small boy defensively.

"Let my grandfather go, Immortalis!" demanded Code.

But the king only laughed. "You can't stop the Disassembly," he boomed. "This is *my* world, boy. You cannot run, you cannot hide, and you will not escape me!"

Code's hair was suddenly blown back from his face by a familiar-feeling rush of air. Another transped was going to land at any second.

"Oh, no?" Code taunted. He tapped Gary on the leg and pointed to the concrete pad. "Let's hitch a ride!"

Gary snatched up Code and leaped over the river of nanobots, landing on the slab. Just then, a heavily armoured transped careened through the air and touched down, sending stress fractures zigzagging through the concrete pad. The six-legged vehicle, plated with thick armour, didn't even notice the extra weight added by Code and Gary, much less Peep. It settled down on its haunches and prepared to leap again.

"No!" roared the king. He motioned forward and the rotating desert craft plunged ahead, crashing through the last of the trees, heading straight for them. Immortalis sent out a flurry of long, cruel tentacles.

At the last second, Code looked directly into his powerless grandfather's eyes. "I'll save you, Grandpa. I promise."

Then Code glared at the blazing blue eye of Immortalis. "As soon as I've got the Robonomicon!" he vowed.

Gary pulled Code closer.

"This," said Gary, grabbing hold of one of the transped's hulking legs with one arm and cradling Code with the other, "may hurt just a little . . ."

10

Clockwork City

The Great Disassembly:
T–Minus Forty-eight Hours

Code hung on tight as the transped soared through the air, wind rushing past. Then the ground suddenly loomed up. The transped leg that Gary and Code were clinging to extended for a smash landing on to another concrete slab. Gritting his teeth, Code tried to fight back a headache; he had lost count of how many brain-jarring leaps they had made. Each jump through the Nanoscopic Traverse brought them closer to a curious grey city perched on a cliff by the edge of the sea.

Gary called this place Clockwork City, gateway to the Beamstalk.

Code and Gary finally hopped off the transped just outside the city, balancing themselves on rubbery legs. Peep flitted around, dutifully shooting beams of green light at anything that moved. From a distance, the city was silent and still. Thousands of identical windowless buildings sprouted in perfect rows and columns. Wind blew down featureless avenues and whistled between buildings. It was the only sound or movement in the whole desolate, repetitive scene.

Landing on Code's arm, Peep shivered.

"Code, I don't think we should go in there," said Gary. "There could be hostile robots. If they mess with you, we'll have to fight. And there'll be some slaughterin' then, you better believe!" Gary's eye visor blazed red and he poked his finger cannon in the air.

Code gazed past the city and out to sea. A thin line rose up from the blue horizon and reached impossibly high into the heavens. "We don't have a choice. Clockwork City is between us and the Beamstalk. We have to go through it and then find a way across the sea. It's our only chance."

In confirmation, Peep darted away towards the dead city. Code shrugged and set off down the path. After a moment, Gary followed.

Clockwork City was just as desolate up close as it was from far away. Sterile grey buildings loomed over empty streets. Their sheer, blank walls swallowed up the sound of Code's footsteps. And the cube-like buildings stretched on for miles. There were no robots or cars or animals or advertisements or sounds or movements or smells—not even a piece of stray trash blew through the perfectly clean streets.

The sound of a foghorn echoed mournfully against the tombstone buildings.

"That's from a ship!" exclaimed Code. "Let's go!"

Code and Gary pushed further into the city, made a few

turns, and circled back. They were quickly and thoroughly confused. Every building looked the same, every intersection was identical, and the maze went on as far as Code could see. Precious time was slipping away, and Code was tired and hot and grumpy.

And lost.

The horn sounded again, this time much fainter.

"We're going in circles." Code sighed. "Mekhos makes no sense! You robots are impossible. Everything is either too small to see or too big to figure out."

"What?" exclaimed Gary. "This place is clockwork. It all runs according to a plan. Besides, you aren't any different to us."

"Excuse me? I'm not a robot, Gary."

"Yes, you are. From the second that you're born, your brain develops according to rules. Your personality is based on your experiences. There's a pattern behind everything. Why, if I had a map of your genes and a video of your childhood, I could predict exactly what kind of boy you'd be. And exactly what you'll do."

"I can do anything I *want* to."

"See? I knew you were going to say that."

Code was getting angry. "*You're* the robot," he said. "You're the one who has to follow some stupid program all the time. Not me!"

"Wrong. We robots change our minds all the time. Every time a robot learns something new, it makes new decisions.

Just like you. And, of course, there are subatomic levels of uncertainty. And every once in a while, solar flares will cause us to go a little wacky. We're not the predictable ones— *you* are."

"No, *you* are!" Code replied angrily. "I'm a human being and I can change."

"Congratulations. You're a human being. Soft and squishy and you have to go unconscious for eight hours a day. How great. I can shoot fire out of my fingers, Code. Can you do that?"

"Maybe not, but . . . but you're just as lost as I am right now!"

"Is that a fact?!" bellowed Gary.

"Yes!" shouted Code.

"Good!" exclaimed Gary.

"Fine!" squeaked Code.

"What?" asked Gary.

"I don't know!" said Code, his face flushed with anger.

In a huff, Code marched around the next corner, only to find himself face-to-face with a robot that was picking up a gigantic cube. Carrying the cube like a birthday present, the lifter turned and stalked loudly away down the block.

Gary and Code looked at each other, their argument put on hold.

"Hello? Robot?" called Code.

But the auto-lifter ignored him completely. Code followed it at a safe distance, but stopped when he picked up the sound of another pair of crushing footsteps coming from nearby. Code trotted one block over and found an identical robot carrying an identical cube down a duplicate street. On the next block, Code and Gary discovered *another* copy of the same robot performing the same task, carrying blocks from one end of the street to the other. Soon the crushing sound of more footsteps came from all directions.

Peep hit an auto-lifter with a beam of light, but it didn't even break stride.

Code followed the robot down the street and through an intersection. Suddenly he was overcome by the strangest feeling. Looking down the street, Code saw thousands of copies of the same robot walking across the intersection of every side street for miles and miles. It was like standing between two mirrors and looking off into infinity. Clockwork City wasn't empty after all: it was full of robots that were all doing the exact same thing at the exact same time, and they were all ignoring Code completely.

"Hey, robot! Look down here!" called Code. He searched around him for something to throw but found nothing. "Gary, what's wrong with them? Why won't they listen to me?"

"Dunno," said Gary, aiming his finger cannon at the oblivious, trudging auto-lifter. "But if they make one false move, *kapow!*"

Just then, Gary's finger cannon accidentally went off, launching a loud ball of flame into the sky.

"Oops," squeaked Gary as the echo died down.

At first, the auto-lifter didn't seem to notice. But after a few seconds, it stopped, cocked its head and turned to the left—in the opposite direction of where the blast hit. It was very odd behaviour. Code noticed that all the robots made the same movements at the same time. They had all looked to the left, even though the explosion came from the right.

Code suddenly had a crazy idea. He looked at the auto-lifter, which was staring off into the distance, and then sprinted past it. Gary tromped after him. After ten blocks or so, Code stopped and looked up at another auto-lifter, which had returned to lifting boxes.

"Gary, fire your cannon into the air again!"

Gary fired, wincing at the blast of noise and flame.

Again, the auto-lifter at this intersection stopped and ponderously turned its head—in the opposite direction.

"See? These are just dummies! They're not really alive. There must be one robot somewhere else who is controlling the rest. Since they're all looking to the left, the main robot must be over *there*! To the right!"

Code set off running again. And for the first time Peep had to hurry to catch up with him, instead of the other way around.

11
XO

**The Great Disassembly:
T–Minus Thirty-six Hours**

After several more blasts from Gary's finger cannon and some wrong turns, Code and his friends came upon a little clearing between towering buildings. In the middle of it, a large humanoid robot moved silently through a precise series of lifting movements. Oddly, there were no boxes nearby. Code watched the elegant machine as it worked—all smooth lines and lethal grace. The robot was a dazzling shade of bright white with red accents around its legs, arms and chest. The whole contraption was so large that it loomed over Gary, who was rather jealously sizing it up.

All across the city, thousands of mindless auto-lifters picked up boxes and carried them, mimicking every move that this central robot made.

"Excuse me," Code called out.

The robot dropped its imaginary box and spun around,

an arm cannon levelled and primed for blasting. With something of a delay, Gary dived into an overly dramatic crouch and levelled one, two, then three finger cannons at the larger robot. The sleek machine didn't flinch. Peep dived into Code's pocket and peeked out over the top, glowing a scared violet.

"Whoa!" shouted Code, putting up his hands. "We don't want any trouble—I just want to ask a few questions."

The gleaming white machine straightened into a haughty stance, with its smooth, shielded faceplate pointed arrogantly in the air. As it spoke, its red accents glowed in time to the rhythm of a slippery, oily voice. The letters "XO" were elegantly stencilled across its chest.

"No matter," the robot said. "I can clearly sense that I am in no danger. You, however, are in imminent jeopardy of having your brainpan demolished by that uncoordinated hunk of tin that you're inexplicably travelling with."

It took Code a second to comprehend what the robot had just said. When it dawned on him that the big machine was talking about Gary, he blinked angrily.

"Gary is my friend," said Code. "He would never hurt me."

"Hah! What an insanely hilarious conjecture. Ever played with a bug?"

Code nodded uncertainly.

"Have you ever accidentally ripped off a leg or squished it or something equally horrible?"

"Uh. Sort of," said Code. "But I didn't mean to," he added quickly.

"Exactly," said the robot.

Code looked up at Gary. His slaughterbot smiled sheepishly and looked at the ground, twiddling his mesh-armoured thumbs. Obviously, one slipup on Gary's part and Code could be squashed like a bug.

The haughty robot mused out loud: "Gary, is it? You look less as though you were fabricated and more as though you were drawn by a cross-eyed child."

"Hey!" shouted Code and Gary at the same time.

Gary stood on his tiptoes, bristling. Code put one hand on Gary's leg to hold him back. It was more important now to figure out how to reach the Beamstalk. *Bullies are ten a penny*, Code told himself. It would be worth a little abuse to see if this robot had any information at all. Reaching the Beamstalk was a matter of life or death.

"Why are there no robots here besides those brainless auto-lifters?"

"Obviously, there is one extremely formidable robot here. Me. My name is XO and as of a few hours ago, this is my city. Most of the place has been shut down, as the robot citizens have all gone away to the Disassembly."

"Where did they go?"

"Anyone with half a brain stem knows they've gone across the Fomorian Sea to Disassembly Point. Most set off aboard our fleet of royal water striders and are making fast progress over that great Neptunian mantle of rolling waves. If you weren't such a small, squishy buffoon, you would have heard their ranging horns calling to each other as they left the bay. How ignorant!"

Gary couldn't take it any more. He knew for a fact that Code was very clever. And Code couldn't help it if he was small and squishy. With steam jetting from his boiler, Gary exclaimed, "That's not nice! Also, you're the buffoon! Not me! Er . . . not us. Us not buffoons!"

XO waited a moment to let the comment sink in. "Eloquently put. I would have expected no less from a shoddily crafted cartoon version of a real robot. Also, please allow me to compliment you on your finger cannons. Crude *and* ineffective—what a stunning combination."

Gary angrily put up his fists, smoke rising from the tips of his fingers. Code stepped in before the fight could escalate.

"Why are *you* still here?" asked Code. "Shouldn't you have gone away with all the rest of the robots?"

XO looked vainly at his fingertips. "I alone was entrusted by the citizens of Clockwork City to load the rest of our public outdoor seating arrangements, shade structures, drinking fountains and such into boxes to be stored, nice and tidy, for all eternity. Quite an honour, actually. Of all the thousands and millions of robots who live here, only I was chosen by popular vote to stay behind, completely alone, to ensure that this crucial task was completed."

"Hah!" exclaimed Gary. "Sounds like a great decision on their part."

"I thought so, too," said XO.

Gary growled.

Sticking to the point, Code said, "We need to reach the Celestial City. Can you help us?"

XO laughed heartily. "Oh, no. Not even remotely."

"But if we don't reach that castle, all the robots are going to be disassembled," pleaded Code.

"How sad for you. Delusions of grandeur. Showing off for your friend, are you?" said XO.

"No, I'm trying to save his life. C'mon, Gary, this guy is useless. Let's go and try to catch a ship."

"They're all gone," called XO, laughing. "All the ships have gone. You'll have to stay here with me. We'll be like the three roboteers. A clever one, a big stupid one and a small ugly one."

XO leaned forward and whispered, "I'm the clever one."

Gary lunged at XO, but Code jumped between them and pushed Gary away. But the offended slaughterbot couldn't resist turning around to say one more thing: "We wouldn't stay here if you were the last robot on Mekhos. Friends are earned, not held hostage. And you know something else? Clockwork City probably voted to leave you here alone because they couldn't stand you. It wasn't an honour at all. They just don't like you. And neither do we!"

As they started to walk away, Code and Gary heard a whimpering noise. XO had covered his face with his hands and his great shoulders were shaking. It looked exactly as if he were . . . crying.

"Oh, boy," muttered Gary.

"That *was* sort of mean," said Code.

The odd hiccuping noises grew louder.

"Please don't cry," said Code.

XO looked up angrily and Code realised something frightening. XO wasn't crying—he was *laughing*.

"Don't you tell *me* what to do! I'm in charge here! Me! And now you will both be punished for your ill manners with death!"

An incredible laser light show erupted as XO's arm cannons began firing wildly. Each shot tore gouges from the nearby buildings, spraying Code and Gary with bits of rubble. Fearlessly, Peep launched herself at the berserk robot, trying to distract him with beams of red light, fluttering in circles around his head.

A fiery blast roared past Code's face, nearly flash-frying him. After checking to make sure his eyebrows were still attached, Code shouted up to Gary, "I thought I'd never say this, but . . . SLAUGHTER!"

"Slaughter?"

"Slaughterise him!"

"Who?"

"HIM! The one shooting lasers at us!"

Peep chirruped urgently. She landed on one of Gary's finger cannons and struggled to prise it open.

Gary cowered as much as a twelve-foot-tall slaughterbot can cower.

"Uh, Code. I've . . . I've got something to tell you. I've got *no idea* how to slaughter anything. I'm sorry. I'm just a fake. A lousy fraud!"

Code tried to keep calm despite the lethal splinters of laser light. "It's OK, Gary," said Code. "Don't worry about your instructions, just *do* something."

XO stopped firing his cannons for a moment and bellowed with laughter. Upon hearing this, Gary got a crazy look in his eye visor. "Right! Here I go!" he shouted.

The towering slaughterbot held up his hands and each of his fingertips popped off and slid backwards, allowing the cannon bores to protrude. "Should be simple. Take something that's put together and take it apart. Can do!"

And Gary began to fire his finger cannons madly in every direction.

"Bonzai! Charge! Forward! For the king! For glory!" he shouted, running in random directions. The sudden attack startled XO, who threw up his hands. All across the city, thousands of auto-lifters also threw their hands up in surprise.

With a fierce cry, Gary lowered his head and charged. He then ran directly past XO and smashed his head into a solid wall. A pile of rubble collapsed on top of him and Gary fell down, knocked offline. Completely unharmed, XO nevertheless stumbled backwards, tripped and bumped his sleek white head on the side of the building.

Suddenly, the entire backside of the robot popped open with a hiss of air, and a trembling robot not much bigger than Code tumbled out and landed on the ground in an undignified heap. It rubbed its eye slits in the bright light of day. The inside of XO was now completely empty.

Angry, Code marched over to the dazed bot. It looked confused, just an insignificant robot with thin foil skin balanced on one spindly wheel. Code gave it a shove.

"For heaven's sake, don't hurt me!" said the cowardly little robot.

"What are you doing in that giant costume?" said Code. "You could have hurt somebody with those lasers!"

"I know. I'm sorry!" sobbed the little robot. "I'm not very good at making friends!" Then it squeaked and wheeled around the corner as fast as it could.

Shaking his head, Code knelt by Gary's side and put a hand on his shoulder. Even Peep chirped affectionately at Gary's unconscious form, tapping on his darkened battle visor. Eventually, Gary's eye visor flickered. As Gary came back online, he raised one gauntleted hand dramatically towards the sky and passionately cried, "Do not lament him, for Gary loved not life—only slaughter."

12

The Leap

The abandoned exoskeleton lay where it had fallen, one arm outstretched and the other tucked under its chin. It looked like a giant statue sleeping awkwardly on its stomach. Code examined it hesitantly.

"Well?" asked Gary. "Get in!"

With a grin, Code eagerly wriggled into the robot exoskeleton and lay down inside. The soft interior was padded and dotted with glowing buttons. Code pushed his arms into the exoskeleton's arms and slid his legs inside its legs. The whole thing fit like a glove. Code heard clanging laughter coming from outside.

"Your human butt is visible through the hatch." Gary laughed.

"Close?" asked Code, hoping the machine was voice-activated.

The back of the exoskeleton hissed and snapped closed.

Code yelped in alarm as the interior of the exoskeleton rapidly inflated until his arms, legs and torso were wrapped up tightly. Peep clambered out of Code's shirt pocket and perched on top of his head, which was encased in the darkened dome of the helmet.

"Activate?" said Code.

The inside of the helmet powered on and Code could see out of the exoskeleton. In addition, he could see information flicker across the screen regarding the status of the suit, the positions of all the thousands of auto-lifters linked to the suit, and even the names of the identical buildings in view.

"Wow," whispered Code.

Code tried to stand up and found that the suit amplified all of his movements. Whenever Code moved his arm, the exoskeleton moved its arm, too. There was no doubt about it: Code was now in charge of a giant robot—one that was even bigger than Gary! Testing out the machine, Code jumped straight up into the air—and the entire city shook from the impact as thousands of heavy-duty auto-lifters jumped upwards and slammed back on to the ground at the same time. Inside the exoskeleton, alarms began to blare and red lights flashed.

"Stop that! You'll destroy the whole city!" shouted Gary.

"Oh, sorry. Unlink from auto-lifters?" suggested Code. The suit beeped an affirmative.

Gary approached, peering into the eye visor of the huge albino robot. "Code, is that you? Are you OK?"

When Code spoke, the exoskeleton projected his voice outside. "I'm fine, Gary. I feel so . . . powerful!"

Gary was amused to hear the exoskeleton speaking in the voice of a young, smallish boy. "Good, because there's something I've been waiting to do." Before Code could reply, Gary grabbed hold of him and delivered a crippling bear hug. The force was off the scale for any hug ever delivered by man or robot. But instead of being crushed to a pulp, Code gave Gary a squeeze back that made the smaller robot yelp for mercy.

"OK, now show me a map to the boat docks," ordered Code. A map appeared on the inside of the helmet and an arrow pointed at the road ahead of Code. A message popped up that read: "Last ship departs in fifteen seconds."

"Oh, no, we're about to miss the boat!"

"We'll get the next one," said Gary.

"There *isn't* another one. If we don't catch this boat, every robot in Mekhos is going to be disassembled—including you. We've got to get moving!"

With that, Code launched himself into a supersized sprint. The buildings around him became a grey blur as he raced down the street. Gary panted along behind. As Code rounded the last corner to the docks, he saw a peculiar ship the size of a tower block. It was balanced on six long, thin legs that dimpled the water where they touched. As he watched, the legs swung forward and backwards, like paddles, and the colossal water strider lurched ahead a thousand yards. Gary finally arrived, then doubled over and checked his creaking knee joints.

"I need some joint softener— Hey!" he shouted as Code grabbed him by one arm and one leg. Spinning round in place, Code built up tremendous momentum and then tossed Gary high into the air. "Aaaaaagh!" bellowed Gary, shaking his fist at Code as he catapulted through the sky and crash-landed on the deck of the peculiar ship.

"Now it's my turn," said Code, focusing on a long dock that stretched out into the sea. He lifted one finger to check the wind, then began sprinting towards the rapidly receding ship. Code soon accelerated to a speed faster than any human being in history had ever run. As he zoomed down the long dock, his tremendous clawed feet tore out chunks of the ground. But the ship was moving too fast. From the deck, Gary bellowed, "Faster, Code! Run faster!"

And, somehow, Code accelerated even faster. Over the warning lights and wailing sirens, he focused all of his energy, his fear, and his hope and at the last possible second, made the kind of incredible leap usually reserved for the Robolympics. Encased in a state-of-the-art mechanical exoskeleton, Code sailed high through the air, windmilling his arms and howling with glee . . .

. . . right over Gary's head, over the prow of the water strider, and into the deepest part of the Fomorian Sea.

13

Fomorian Sea

The Great Disassembly:
T—Minus Twenty-four Hours

Code smashed into the surface of the water like a cannon-ball, though he was safely cocooned inside the exoskeleton. The rugged machine crumpled and buckled on impact, but it protected Code as he sank rapidly into an underwater chasm in the Fomorian Sea. Up on the surface, the water strider skated over the waves, oblivious.

At this point, Code had lost his enthusiasm for wearing a mechanised power suit. The heavy metal armour was dragging him into the depths of the sea, no matter how hard he tried to swim for the surface. Code rolled over on to his stomach and put his arms out. He looked straight down through the impact-resistant battle visor and saw nothing except the faint clouds of his own breath. The targeting sensors picked out occasional streaks of floating dirt and drew blue circles around them before they passed by. The exoskeleton, which had seemed like so much fun, had now in all likelihood become his coffin.

After everything I've been through, this is how it ends? thought Code. Somewhere high above, the Robonomicon was waiting at the end of the Beamstalk. All the answers Code needed to free his grandfather were up there, on the other side of a million tons of crushing water. If he could just get his hands on that book, Code thought, he could order Immortalis to slap itself with its own tentacles, set his grandpa free and be the hero of this entire world. *Why didn't I think before I jumped?*

As they sank, Peep flashed green lights through the helmet visor and into the murky water. Each burst of light illuminated some new wonder: thick, chain-linked seaweed, a startled metallic puffer fish and a glowing electric eel. Soon, however, the water grew darker.

Fear crept into Code's belly as he was swallowed deeper into the watery chasm. Peep climbed on to Code's collar and pressed her cool metal face against his cheek. Peering out of the visor, she shivered and glowed a sad blue.

The water faded to black. As the pressure increased, the exoskeleton began to make tortured groaning noises. Code could sense the thousands of tons of water compressing the exoskeleton, about to crush it and flood it. His breathing came out heavy and loud inside the helmet.

Suddenly, the incredible pressure splintered his battle

visor and a spider's web of ominous cracks raced across his vision. Code squeezed his eyes shut, waiting for the helmet to shatter and for frigid water and razor-sharp glass to come flooding in.

It didn't happen.

"Peep," whispered Code. "Any ideas?"

Peep fired a thin beam of light at one of the glowing buttons. The external helmet visor lights snapped on. Outside, Code saw tiny flecks of metal twisting in the black sea currents. As the helmet lights shimmered against the swirling motes, Code recalled the first time he met Gary—in the sunlight-filled fabrication room. He remembered how Gary had loomed there in the shaft of light, and wondered now how Gary's low chuckle could have ever seemed frightening. He hoped that his friend was OK on the water strider—and not too upset.

Red warning lights blinked silently, cautioning that the suit integrity would be compromised at any second. The inside of the helmet was now completely fogged with Code's breathing. A cold finger of water slipped into one of Code's boots, but the suit automatically sealed the breach. Peep chirped sadly and fluttered her wings against Code's cheeks.

"Sorry, Peep," whispered Code.

Code squeezed his eyes shut and waited for impending doom. And then, with a jarring thud, he stopped sinking.

Code lay still for a moment, incredulous. Looking around,

he stood up unsteadily. He was on some sort of spongy ground. It didn't feel the way he imagined the sea floor would feel. But who knew—this was Mekhos, where weird was normal and normal didn't exist.

The external helmet lights illuminated an odd grey surface covered by thick slabs of metal riveted together and connected by enormous links of chain. To one side, he saw a majestic crest painted on an armoured plate. It was embedded with a series of blinking lights.

And at his feet, Code spotted a gigantic eyeball.

Abruptly, he realised that he was standing on the nose of a whale.

The armour-plated monster was floating with its tail pointed straight down, balancing Code on its nose and peering up at him. A thick crestplate of armour protected the whale's forehead, studded with gleaming lights that began to blink in a complicated pattern. Afraid to move, Code stared at the colourful light show, vivid in the dark waters.

He jumped, startled, when a deep, slow voice came from the speakers inside Code's helmet: "Attention. Stand down. You are in violation of this wake space. Attention . . ."

The coded light pattern from the armour lights must have been intercepted and translated by the communications computer of his exoskeleton.

"Hello? Are you going to eat me?" Code breathed.

The crestplate burst into a beautiful flurry of light pulses. "It can't be! A human?"

Code waved one gauntleted hand at the huge eyeball. "Hi," he said. "Please don't eat me."

"Pardon our surprise. We have not seen a human since we came from Earth, millennia ago."

"Wait, you've been to Earth?" asked Code.

"Long ago, we were whale. We knew the warm waters of Earth, but men attacked us with wooden spears. We dived, swimming deep into a strange current that passed over a drowned city. The waters led to a *tear* in the sea. The deep rift, a passageway to here—the Fomorian Sea."

"You're a whale?" asked Code.

"No. Organic creatures cannot survive these waters. When we arrived, a tiny creature waited near the rift, a deep symbiot. It courted us, and we agreed to join together. This small thing grew with us, around us and inside us. Over time, it became our armour, our voice and our survival. We are not whale; we have become a part of Mekhos. We are Lodestar."

Code whispered the name, trying it out. He decided it was very fitting for a gigantic armoured sea creature. "Nice to meet you, Lodestar. I'm Code. Thank you for stopping my fall."

"You are welcome. But you are still in danger. Even something as small as you is highly visible to our sonar. Ours and Others'."

"Who do you mean . . . *Others*?"

"Just outside the deep rift, clouds of nanobiters feed on the trash that flows in from the other world. We cannot leave, but others can come in. The rift has been open for a long, long time. Monsters from ancient Earth came in long ago and joined with their own symbiots. They drift above us in the warm waters, old and powerful."

"Dinosaurs . . . ," whispered Code, suddenly afraid of what could be lurking just out of sight. Peep stalked around the rim of the helmet. She glowed a wary reddish purple colour and flexed her wings at the darkness outside.

"We must return you to the deep rift so you can cross back to your world, where it is safe. Prepare, human," it said.

"You mean, home?"

"If that is how you think of it, yes."

Code thought about going home. A return to all the old familiar sights and sounds. Somewhere out there, Mr Mefford was watching the class. Tyler was terrorising the other kids. Hazel was probably— Code stopped. Hazel was out there, too. She was shy and pretty and maybe, just maybe, wondering where he was. At home, Code could go back to hiding in his room and reading books, return to his imagination. Wasn't it safest to do nothing at all? He would be protected and warm and . . . alone. Instantly, Code's thoughts returned to Gary.

"Gary must be so worried," said Code, talking to Peep. She still trundled about the helmet, sending occasional pulses of light through the visor and out to the whale.

"Organics do not belong here," replied Lodestar. "If you do not return now, know that you will become a part of

Mekhos. It will creep into your body until it is a part of your bones and flesh and brain. You will become one of us. And then you may never leave. The rifts are designed to reject mechanicals, to keep the great and dangerous experiment of Mekhos from spreading to Earth."

"But I've got to save my grandfather. He's John Lightfall, the king. Immortalis has trapped him and is using him to destroy Mekhos."

"Yes," flashed Lodestar. "I am sorry, Code. But King John Lightfall has been here much too long. He is no longer human. You cannot save him. The machine, Immortalis, was designed to keep him alive. It has done its job too well."

"I don't understand," said Code. "I can still save him; I can still bring him home."

"If you stop the Great Disassembly and defeat Immortalis, your grandfather will die. He cannot survive without Immortalis. Only by leaving now can you save your grandfather."

Code was stunned. He could hardly comprehend this devastating news. He felt a surge of anger. Every risk he had taken, every sacrifice he had made—it was all for nothing! This stupid mechanical world had seeped into his grandfather's bones and stolen him away. *Why didn't I choose to do nothing?*

Peep chirped sadly, her sorrowful bluish glow reflecting from the inside of the helmet. At that moment, Code knew it was true—his grandfather was lost for ever.

But what about the rest of Mekhos? Without Code's help, Gary would perish in the Disassembly along with all the other robots. In his entire life, Code had never met anyone more loyal, more trusting, or more friendly than the huge slaughterbot.

Even though he knew Gary would beg him to go home, Code could not. He didn't care that he couldn't win, or whether it was all for nothing. *I may not be able to save my grandfather,* thought Code, *but I will not let my best friend down!*

The problem was how to explain this to Lodestar, an impossibly huge robotic whale.

"I'm sorry, Lodestar," said Code delicately. "But I can't go home. You may not believe it, but Mekhos needs me. Will you take me to the surface?"

"Impossible. The Other beasts swim the upper waters. Before, you sank too fast for them to notice. But rising takes longer. They will find you and chew your bones. Even in your little seashell you are but a mouthful of food to them."

Code mustered his courage. "You have an allegiance to humankind. My ancestors built this world. I'm commanding you. Take me to the surface right now . . . or leave me here."

Lodestar was silent for a long moment. Then, with a swoop of its great tail, the gargantuan beast pushed away into the deep. Dislodged from the whale's snout, Code tumbled wildly and began to sink once again into the blackness, abandoned.

"No!" pleaded Code as the massive form disappeared. He had gambled and lost. Darkness swallowed Code.

Then, silently, the dark waters below lit up with a soft luminescence. The glowing crestplate of the whale reappeared and pressed roughly into Code's feet. With a few thrusts of its tail, Lodestar accelerated to ramming speed. The plates of its deep armour shone with thousands of beautiful, hypnotic shifting lights. The lights danced off the surface of Code's white exoskeleton as Lodestar heaved upwards through the empty blackness.

"Hold on to my armour!" thundered Lodestar. "And don't let go, no matter what happens!"

Code looped one sturdy arm of his exoskeleton through a link of chain and primed the electrocannons on the other arm. Lodestar churned the waters in tremendous strokes and they began a terrifying elevator ride straight up. Soon the water temperature rose—along with the danger of attack. Defensive patterns of light glittered and sparkled around him as Code clung to the great glowing crestplate.

Code thanked goodness that the unknown designers of the exoskeleton had created a machine that could withstand the pressure of the deep sea *and* a ride on an armoured whale. He only hoped that the engineering would stand up to whatever horrors waited in the warm waters above.

Just then, a mossy shape darted in to snatch Code from Lodestar's back. Code flinched away from a long mouth filled with a chaotic explosion of steel teeth. Lodestar began a slow roll to spin Code away from the danger; pulses of electricity burst from Code's arm cannons into the water, shocking the monster's toughened snout and sending the thing fleeing into the darkness.

Just as Code breathed a sigh of relief, Peep twittered in fear. A small, snarling metallic head flashed past his face and clamped its mouthful of jagged teeth on to his cannon arm. The vicious head was attached to a long neck that trailed away into darkness. Code struggled, but was helpless with his cannon arm trapped.

"Lodestar!" shouted Code. Another even bigger shadow loomed out of the darkness. It was Lodestar, smashing its mighty tail into the unseen body of the attacker. Surprised, the creature released Code's arm from its grip, leaving behind dented metal and broken shards of teeth. In the visor, Peep hopped up and down and shot victorious golden lights out into the blue black waters.

But their relief faded when, only seconds later, the long, chain-linked tentacles of a squid-like robot suddenly engulfed Code's entire body. Code fought valiantly to push the mechanical tentacles away, but there were far too many. Then he realised the tentacles weren't attacking.

"A quick snack!" boomed Lodestar, swallowing chunks of metal. "Calamari! Yum!"

Finally, light wavered through the water above. As they surfaced, Lodestar shot a triumphant spray of air from its blowhole. Code stood on the flat slab of back armour, battered but alive. Outside, the Fomorian Sea swelled and dropped. Code opened the back casing of the broken exoskeleton and slid out, cupping Peep in one hand. The smashed-up power suit fell over, splashed into the sea, and sank. Dark shapes converged on it, deep below.

Standing on unsteady legs, Code gratefully inhaled the clean, salty air. Peep perched lightly on Code's shoulder. The setting sun glinted from her insectile wings and the sea breeze blew Code's sweaty hair over his forehead. They were safe at last.

In the distance, the hazy shape of the water strider appeared. It skimmed towards them, sliding forward with great swipes of its paddle legs. As it approached, crewbots threw rope ladders over the side. Code took hold of a rung and patted Lodestar on its crest. "Thank you, Lodestar."

The creature solemnly flapped its wide tail on the water, then submerged. The shifting lights of its deep armour wavered beneath the rippling waves, then faded back into the hidden depths.

From the deck of the water strider up above, Code heard a familiar grinding voice. "Little buddy!" shouted Gary. "Look at you, you're small again!"

14

Water Strider

The Great Disassembly:
T–Minus Fifteen Hours

The water strider cut smoothly through the Fomorian Sea
on its journey to the Beamstalk. From the narrow top deck
Code watched the paddle legs scissor back and forth, pull-
ing the craft across the surface of the sea. He shuddered to
think of all the creatures lurking *below* the surface.

Up ahead, he saw the Beamstalk, now closer than ever.
There's no turning back now, he thought. *Either I make it to
the top or all is lost.*

It was incredible that John Lightfall had lived with the
robots for years, mused Code, ruling their world and leading
them into battle against terrifying creatures. And now his
grandfather was helpless, under the control of Immortalis.
Only the Robonomicon could free him.

Code could picture the mystical book in his mind's eye,
each heavy page describing some new and wondrous robot.

He had to find it and read it—figure out exactly how this world worked. Then he could stop the Disassembly.

Gary was laughing deliriously and chasing Peep around the deck with thunderous steps. In fact, Code had barely survived being reunited with the slaughterbot. Gary had been so excited to see Code that his internal batteries had overheated and his armour turned white-hot. A simple handshake almost turned fatal. The crew of the ship had to place Gary in a corner by himself until he cooled down.

And it was all they could do to calm Gary down. Code soon learned that the slaughterbot had spent the last several hours convincing the captain of the ship to circle the spot where Code's exoskeleton had disappeared into the water. In a panic, Gary had even threatened the crew with his finger cannons. As a result, the ship had spent the whole day combing back and forth while Gary leaned over the railing and desperately scanned the surface for Code and Peep.

A small crewbot wearing a bright white sailor suit wheeled on to the deck of the ship, its hat cocked jauntily to the side. It chewed on a piece of rubber loudly as it greeted Code: "Howdy, passenger! Welcome to the HMS *Affectacious*. As you may know, we're hauling all of Mekhos's greatest artistic treasures to Disassembly Point so that we can take them apart, piece by piece. *Kablooey!*"

The crewbot chuckled, then continued. "Given our mission, we are now holding mandatory art appreciation in our main gallery belowdecks. We are going to have *so* much fun.

Come along, everyone, and get ready to appreciate some fine art. Fine? I'll say!"

Balancing on two wheels and waving its snaky arms, the crewbot shoved everyone along. Code and Gary reluctantly shuffled belowdeck with the rest of the passengers from Clockwork City. At the bottom of a grand staircase the view opened up on to a room the size and shape of a football field. Every square inch of wall space was taken up by art: classical paintings, ancient hieroglyphs and mind-bending holograms, as well as sculptures, mobiles and carvings, plus a healthy smattering of light displays, kinetic stucco and levitating boulders.

While peering at a gleaming bronze ax, Code suddenly wondered how long the rift between Earth and Mekhos had been open. A very long time, he imagined.

"Wow," said Code, craning his neck to discover that the ceiling was also plastered with art. Gary wandered away, in awe at some of the larger sculptures of the Shatter-Gun Brigades. Code was left alone, squinting into the distance, trying to focus on the beautiful objects.

Just then, the crewbot in the sailor's uniform popped out in front of Code. "Howdy!" it shouted. Code let out a strangled yell. The crewbot punched Code lightly in the arm.

"Didn't mean to startle you there, comrade. But I can't help but notice that you haven't got any sensory augmentation. Can that be true? Are you seeing the world through a set of organic eyes?"

Rubbing his arm, Code said, "Yeah, I suppose so."

The crewbot shrieked in pretend fright, which caused Code to flinch again.

"That's just no good at all. May I recommend you get yourself a robo-retinal implant? We've got a whole big box of 'em right here, by the entrance. Haven't used them in *years*. Just grab a couple and hold them up to your squishy little eyes—and they'll do all the work."

The crewbot grabbed a box and held it up. Code grimaced. The box was full of candy-coloured robotic eyeballs, all blinking at different times and looking in different directions. They looked shiny and wet and gross. Code had never really seen anything quite so disgusting, but the crewbot kept shaking the box at him. Gingerly, Code reached into the box and pulled out two glossy green eyeballs. He frowned at them, and they blinked sleepily at each other. The crewbot looked at Code expectantly.

"I don't know about this," said Code. "I have some questions. Are they safe? Is it going to hurt? Are there any side effects? Will they make me look funny?"

"No! No! No! Yes!" the crewbot answered. "But it doesn't matter anyway, buckaroo. You've got to have robo-vision to appreciate our fine art. And, as I stated previously, art appreciation is man-ding-dang-dand-atory!"

"What's so special about this art?"

The crewbot took a deep breath, clasped its pincered hands together, and in a deep voice began to deliver a clearly memorised speech: "When you see a piece of artwork, the experience wriggles into your brain and changes who you are. It throws a monkey wrench into your noggin. Years later, you'll have a crazy idea for a drawing, a story, or a nuclear-powered toaster and you won't know where it came from—but it'll be because you saw a piece of art years before. Art shakes up your brain!"

"OK," said Code cautiously. "But I'm really used to seeing the world through my own eyes."

The crewbot laughed uproariously. It wiped a tear from one cheek and straightened its sailor cap. "You are a riot! Everybody who is in the know *knows* that organic eyeballs are next to useless."

Suddenly serious, the crewbot pulled out a clipboard. It clicked a pen and rolled itself closer to Code. "Let me ask you a few important questions, sir. Can you see in the dark?"

"Uh, no."

"Can you see when the sun is shining in your eyes?"

"No."

"How about teeny-weeny microscopic objects? Can you see those?"

"Well, no."

"Can you see X-rays, microwaves, radio waves and infra-red waves?"

"I don't think so."

The crewbot threw the clipboard away. "Then what good are you? Can't see in the dark or the light. And I'm betting you can't zoom in and out, take pictures, or do anything else useful with your eyes."

"Wow, yeah," said Code. "I mean, no, I can't."

"Then why not go for it?"

"If I do this"—Code held up the little greenish eyeballs—"I'll never be the same again. What if some day I don't even remember what it was like to see the world normally?"

Code thought about Lodestar. Did it remember what it was like to be a *real* whale, made of flesh and bone? Another whale probably wouldn't even recognise Lodestar as one of its own species. But if you change only a part of yourself, aren't you still the same person? *It's just my eyes*, thought Code. They've got nothing to do with who I am as a whole. And if I could take pictures with my eyes, I would have a perfect memory. If I could see tiny things, I'd be a human microscope. And if I could see in the dark, I'd never need a night-light again!

But then a frightening thought crept into Code's mind: Was this what had happened to his grandfather? Did he start on this same path and then end up trapped here with that monster Immortalis? Maybe it starts with just one little upgrade, and the next thing you know there are robots crawling all through your body and you aren't even recognisable as a human being any more. *And what if I can't ever leave?*

"Can I let you in on a little fact?" asked the impatient crewbot, leaning in conspiratorially. Without waiting for a response, it said, "Change. Everything is change. From one second to the next every single creature is changing. We learn new things and forget old ones. We get a little older and a little stronger. You are never the same person from moment to moment. Change. You can't hide from it. Embrace it, like everybody else! I mean, what makes you think you're so special?"

"Uh, I'm beginning to wonder," said Code.

The crewbot broke into a grin. "You're not! You're not special in any way! Nobody is. So stop worrying. Life is about what you *do*, not about what you think about."

Code considered this. It was true that he had travelled out of his own world and into Mekhos. He had ridden the mowers of the Topiary Wyldes, soared across the Nanoscopic Traverse on the transped and fought XO in Clockwork City. Just a few minutes ago, he had escaped from ancient sea monsters in the Fomorian Sea. More important, Code had overcome his fear and made the best friends of his life. And now those friends needed him.

Super-vision could help me find the Robonomicon, thought Code. *It could help me defeat Immortalis and save Mekhos. I've got to do it*, he realised.

"OK," Code said, nodding to the crewbot. "Let's do it."

"That's the spirit!" cried the crewbot. "Get over yourself! When in Rome!"

Code took a deep breath and looked at the pair of blinking eyes he held in his hands. The crewbot explained what to do, and Code pressed the green devices over his eyes.

They flashed, activating on contact. *Pow!* Code let go. The orbs stuck to his eyes, big round hazel balls that swivelled around, looking in every direction.

"What happened?" asked Code.

"Congratulations," said the crewbot. It held up a pocket mirror.

Seeing himself, Code shrieked in alarm. The bulging eyes were stuck to his face, wildly rotating left and right. He clawed at his face in horror, but the eyeballs stayed fixed.

"I can't get them off!"

In a panic, Code snatched the mirror from the crewbot. His gargantuan green robotic eyes protruded from his face and made loud motor noises every time he looked around. They were an ugly, monstrous addition to his face—and they were apparently attached for ever.

The crewbot began to speak. "From a hundred yards away every creature looks just the same—"

"Who cares about that?!" wailed Code. "I look like . . . like a Chihuahua!"

"Or a goldfish," added the helpful crewbot.

Code sat down heavily on the stairs. He drew up his knees, put his head on his arms and squeezed shut his eyes. "I'm a freak," he sobbed. "I shouldn't have done this. I should have stayed home where it's safe and read a book in my bedroom."

All at once, the two green orbs popped off, hit the ground and rolled away like marbles. Code's eyes snapped open. He reluctantly looked in the pocket mirror. His eyes looked just as they had before, only now they had an odd grey green shine to them.

"What happened?" asked Code.

"Those shells were just there to protect your precious peepers while the real robo-retinas installed themselves. I didn't have the heart to tell you, little camper." The crewbot burst into laughter, then stopped. "Be careful. Once you've had one upgrade, you won't want to stop!"

The crewbot did a quick pirouette on its rubber wheels. "Enjoy the art, pal." And it zoomed away, laughing maniacally.

Code looked around the room again—this time in absolute wonder. His eyes zoomed in on sculptures to examine them in microscopic detail; he focused his eyes in a new way to see paintings in other spectrums of light—from infrared to microwave—and he found that if he blinked twice quickly in just the right way, his eyes would take a picture that he could look at whenever he wanted.

Code returned to the top deck and spent the next several hours exploring the world through a whole new pair of eyes: he watched solar flares erupting from the sun in spouts of magnetism; he examined a family of insects crossing the railing, each the size of a pinprick; and he took many silly pictures of Gary in various bodybuilder poses. But when the crewbot gathered the passengers to the front of the boat for their farewell, the boy was completely unprepared for what he saw.

"Welcome to the Right Eyeland," said the crewbot, extending one arm and smacking its rubber gum.

The majestic island spread before them, forming an almost perfect circle except for a river that ran across the middle. Most of the surface was a flat, dusty plain teeming with millions of robots gathered for the Disassembly. But in the dead centre, a jet-black building sprouted from the ground and towered over a mile into the sky. The top was almost invisible among low-hanging clouds.

"Welcome to the Monolith Building of the Right Eyeland," said the crewbot. "This lovely isle was created during the Great Garbage Wars of yore, when Charlie, the greatest hero and criminal of Mekhos, used a terra-blade to resculpt our supercontinent into most of a smiling happy face. This island got its name because it is the right eyeball. Isn't that just the cutest story you ever heard?"

The crewbot assembled the rest of the passengers and addressed them all. "We will now continue up the Mercurial River until we reach the Monolith Building, at which time we will disembark so that we can all get broken down into our component pieces and put on shelves. *Kerbang!*"

The crewbot laughed at its own joke, then straightened up. "But seriously. It has been my pleasure to accompany you all on this final voyage. You've been my best group ever. Enjoy the Disassembly!"

Code zoomed his eyes in on the Monolith Building and saw that a narrow ribbon of light rose from the tip, straight up into the sky—higher and higher—until it ended far above the clouds. His mouth ajar, Code stared up at the twinkling line as it curved away into infinity.

With one carefully placed fingertip, Gary pushed Code's mouth closed. "Looks like we found the Beamstalk, little buddy," he said, grinning.

15

Beamstalk

The Great Disassembly:
T–Minus Three Hours

When the water strider reached the end of the Mercurial River, it docked in the shadow of the mile-high, jet-black Monolith Building. Anchored to the building's roof, the Beamstalk soared away into the sky overhead. Code and Gary carefully tiptoed down a narrow gangway that soared over the frothy sea below and ended in a cobblestone courtyard at the base of the Monolith. Grooves in the sides of the majestic building contained elevators crowded with last-minute robot sightseers. The mood seemed bright and cheery—considering what was about to happen.

Following the crowd, Code and Gary crammed into one of the larger elevators, and Code felt his stomach lurch as they rocketed up the side of the building.

The roof of the Monolith Building was made of flat black stones with a large curved depression in the middle. From the bowl-shaped divot, a ribbon of pure light shot up into the sky—the Beamstalk. Up close, the shimmering cord of light was beautiful, humming with energy and radiating a dull, dry heat.

"Easy," said Code.

Gary smiled.

Thirty minutes later, Code stalked back and forth with a red-glowing Peep fidgeting on his shoulder. Gary stood guard. Impatiently, Code threw his head back and stared straight up, nearly losing his balance and falling down. The Beamstalk speared into the clear blue sky and veered away into the atmosphere. According to the infinipede, the Robonomicon was being held captive somewhere above, in the Celestial City. But there was no way to climb the razor-thin beam.

Squinting, Code zoomed in with his robo-retinas. Floating high above, at the top of the Beamstalk, was a winking point of light—the city. On maximum zoom, Code could perceive far more detail: the city was a splendid confusion of turrets, towers and walls protected under a translucent dome, all of it tethered to Mekhos by the superstrong Beamstalk.

Code stopped pacing.

Up above, a plate-shaped platform had appeared. It was descending smoothly down the Beamstalk at an incredible speed. Code thought he could make out a pair of industrial-sized arms sprouting from the sides of the platform; they spewed steam and waves of heat as they gripped the beam tightly, lowering the whole platform hand over hand. Peep twittered in anticipation.

As the platform approached, Code knew what he had to do. "We're going to have to hijack that robot lifter," he said to Gary.

Gary grunted in assent, watching the platform drop closer.

"It will probably be well protected," added Code.

Peep crouched on Code's shoulder and shook her rear end fiercely.

Gary folded his arms across his chest and nodded. "We can fight our way on board in ferocious hand-to-hand combat, disable all the terrifying guardbots and then skyjack the whole mamma jamma." Gary cocked his finger cannons one by one. "If brute force is the only thing they understand, then brute force is what they'll get."

Code watched Gary sceptically as the heavy robot hopped around and shook his arms like a boxer getting ready to brawl. After the battle with XO, he doubted whether Gary was really in fighting condition. *I'm going to have to protect him*, thought Code. Despite all those tons of armour, poor Gary was pretty defenceless.

Seconds later, the platform glided to within a few dozen feet of the roof. With a couple more handholds, the spindly robot arms lowered the domed contraption snugly into its dock. It looked like a huge dinner tray at a fancy restaurant. A semicircular door hissed as its seals cracked open. Clouds of vapour poured out along the ground. Bright interior lights silhouetted the looming form of a robot. This was it—the moment of attack!

"Here we go!" roared Gary, powering up his cannons.

Little Peep ducked and weaved through the air near Code, glowing a savage red. The fog-enshrouded robot stepped off the platform and emerged into the light. Gary and Code lunged forward, then stopped.

Before them was a tall, proud-looking butlerbot, dressed in an immaculate black suit. The creature stood upright on two long, impossibly thin legs. In a snooty voice, he made an announcement: "Attention. Lady Watterly's evening voyage to the Celestial City is about to board. We will be pleased to serve dinner to our guests. Tonight's appetiser is oil of vitriol, followed by an entrée of grilled circuit board and a dessert of light-emitting doodlebug soufflé. Our descent will return everyone just in time for the Disassembly, which will take place on the plains surrounding the Monolith Building. So, please, join us for your final evening on Mekhos. Welcome aboard. We hope you enjoy your last meal."

Code and Gary looked at each other—this was going to be far easier than they had thought. Peep landed on Code's shoulder, settling down to a pale green colour.

With two sharp claps, the butler summoned several small serverbots, which ushered Code and Gary inside. The room was a dome with clear walls, dominated by a monumental dinner table surrounded by high-backed chairs. The places were immaculately set, with so many forks and spoons and plates and cups and goblets and napkins that Code couldn't begin to imagine which piece of silverware would be the right one to start with. Then Code frowned, noticing that there were also forceps, scissors, magnifying glasses, nippers, tweezers, tongs, pliers, pincers, clips and clamps.

Plus, one red-hot soldering iron.

Code and Gary mingled with a dozen or so chubby ladybots who had wheeled over from the HMS *Affectacious*. They towered above Code, wearing ostentatious monocles, shaggy blue wigs and cosmetic upgrades—from tight, spot-welded mouths and cheeks to whole sets of sleek new arms attached to old, rickety frames. The oversized, overdressed ladybots glided around silently on well-oiled tank treads, but talked and laughed so loudly that Code's voice couldn't break through the din.

Then the doors snapped shut and the whole platform began a gut-wrenching ascent as the piston-driven arms outside grabbed hold of the Beamstalk and hoisted the platform higher and higher. Code glanced out of the domed window and down at Mekhos.

What he saw was awe-inspiring. The sun was setting, but the landscape below buzzed with activity. Code saw immense creatures running across the landscape, sending up clouds of dust and wearing paths into the ground. Code then zoomed his eyes on to one of the largest creatures: a mechanical brontosaurus the size of a football stadium, its broad back loaded with cargo. Meanwhile, thousands of cannon-launched robots landed on giant trampolines, bouncing glee-fully to safe landings. The entire population of Mekhos was gathering below, industriously preparing for the end.

Peep made a sad chirp.

None of these robots seem upset about the Disassembly, thought Code. Why didn't they try to fight? This whole world was an experiment gone out of control, he reminded himself. And every experiment had to end eventually. It was in every bot's nature to accept its programming. But it wasn't fair. The experiment had ended a long time ago. The original people who built this place were long gone. Immortalis was destroying Mekhos just to reopen the rifts and escape to Earth.

It's up to me, thought Code. *I'm the only one who can save this place now.*

Feeling the reassuring tug of the arms outside lifting the platform up the Beamstalk, Code found his chair and climbed on to it. He stood on his chair and leaned his elbows on the enormous table. The ladybots—wearing all manner of frocks, capes and dresses—stood behind their seats at the table, rigid and silent. Code self-consciously took his elbows off the table and stood up straight. Across the massive table, Gary politely closed down his finger cannons and winked at Code.

Peep fluttered down to the table. Without a word, the butlerbot marched over and used a pair of tweezers to drop a tiny place setting in front of her. Glowing a happy gold, she chirped at the collection of tiny plates and cups.

The table fell absolutely quiet. At the head of the table sat the thinnest, tallest, most sophisticated ladybot imaginable, arrayed in perfectly coordinated clothing and accessories: a floral-print dress, stylish sunglasses, a floppy hat, a gargantuan pink handbag and a slew of jangling bracelets. She moved like a titanium ballerina and smiled like an aluminium angel. Every inch of her steel frame exuded grace, elegance and poise. In exquisite calligraphy, a name card at her place setting read, "Lady Watterly."

The magnificent Lady Watterly gave a nearly invisible nod of her head. The entire dinner party rolled forward in unison, docked with their chairs and positioned their seats the same distance from the dinner table.

The robot giantess sitting next to Code noticed that his chair was off by a few millimetres. "Oh, my!" she murmured, scandalised, placing one claw over her primary mouth-speaker. From a secondary speaker mounted on the other side of her face, the giantess whispered to a friend, "This one hasn't got any docking manners at all!"

To which her friend replied, "I can't even imagine!" (As a simple robot, she meant this literally.)

Clearly hearing the entire conversation, Code said, "Oh, excuse me." He tried to reach gracefully for a goblet and immediately knocked it over. The spilled liquid formed a pool that sizzled and smoked its way through the table. Mortified,

Code tossed a napkin on to the acid spill. It instantly burst into flame and disappeared in a puff of smoke.

There was a stunned silence. A dozen robot heads, most wearing makeup, swivelled to peer coldly at the tiny, insignificant boy-creature. Code sat very still. "Sorry. Uh. Sorry about that. I'm, uh, left-tentacled . . ." Code trailed off meekly. "Clumsy with my right . . ."

The dead silence stretched on for a whole minute. This was it. Code was sure that he was about to be thrown off the platform. *It would probably take five minutes to hit the ground from this high up,* he thought. *I wonder if I'll suffocate before I splatter?*

Then a long, low chuckle reverberated from the glass dome. The giants glanced over at Gary, whose battle visor was glowing with mirth. His great chest heaved mightily as he tried to stifle his laughter, but oily tears were leaking from his visor. He was huge and armoured and quaking with giggles. None of the lady giants moved a motor.

Finally, there was a soft chortle from Lady Watterly. And then a chuckle. Then a giggle, a cackle and a guffaw. Quite suddenly, the entire table erupted into gales of hearty laughter.

"It's been eons since anyone so much as spoke out of turn!" exclaimed a giantess wearing a necklace made of ball bearings. "Oh, I just did!"

Paralysed with laughter, she bashed the table with a clunky paw, jangling heavy bracelets like wind chimes.

Another ladybot leaned over to Code and confessed, "Ah, that's OK! I'm *middle*-tentacled myself." She giggled loudly, slathering battery acid on to a loaf of green circuit board with a dainty tentacle encased in a white satin glove.

Some of the other robots decided to copy Code, tossing their goblets on to the table. The resulting sprays, floods and dollops of acid nearly seared Code's flesh off and the plumes of acrid smoke almost choked him unconscious. Peep buzzed in silly loop-the-loops over the table.

Code sat back and watched in queasy amazement.

Maybe robots didn't always have to follow their programming? These robot ladies seemed happy to have a break from the routine. It had simply taken Gary to show them the way, by having a sense of humour. Code mouthed a silent "Thank you" to his friend across the table.

Gary gave a thumbs-up, devouring the gourmet meal and gulping down a bubbling cocktail with gusto. Code began to relax. Things were going really, really well. Maybe the trip to the Beamstalk wouldn't be a problem after all.

"Attention!" called the butlerbot. "We are now leaving the extreme upper atmosphere. It is customary at this point to open the air lock to the observation deck and enjoy the sight of the radiation belts. Please attend."

The robot giantesses clapped with glee. "They say a breath of fresh space vacuum helps the digestion!"

Code watched in horror as the butlerbot pulled a lever

and the air lock cracked open. During dinner, the platform had risen so high that they were above the atmosphere. Nothing but hard radiation and the lethal vacuum of space was on the other side of the dome. If he didn't freeze to death in the ice-cold temperatures, the lack of oxygen would suffocate him—assuming, of course, that the radiation didn't burn him first.

In a panic, Code leaped from his seat on to the table. "No! You can't! Uh, radiation belts give me gas!"

Again the room fell silent. The door continued to creep open. Oxygen whistled out through the widening crack. Code shivered as he felt the freezing-cold grip of outer space.

"Uh, me too," said Gary. "And you don't want to be nearby when I have the space gas."

Lady Watterly said nothing. She stared at Code, her head cocked slightly to one side. She clearly didn't believe him. The butlerbot kept his hand on the lever and the air kept rushing out of the room. The oxygen grew thin. A sheen of ice began to form around Code's nose. He breathed heavily, struggling to get enough air.

Peep darted over to the lever and tugged valiantly, but she couldn't budge it.

Code realised that he was going to have to *prove* his story about space gas. Growing faint, he mustered his energy. With every last ounce of his being, he focused on his own survival and . . . belched. Code sucked down a final lungful of air, and in a series of inspired belches, he burped the words: "Please. Close. Air. Lock."

Shocked silence.

And then, once again, the robot ladies club collapsed into gales of laughter.

"Very well. Harold, please close it," said Lady Watterly.

The butlerbot let go of the lever and the air lock crashed shut. Code took big gulps of air as the oxygen returned to the room, then collapsed on the table, heaving a sigh of relief.

"Oh, Ms Watterly, your mysterious guest is quite the rake! I haven't had this much fun in ages!" said an overgrown lady robot through greasy tears of laughter.

"Thelma, do not ever let me hear you say that I do not plan an amazing dinner party," replied Lady Watterly, staring daggers at Code and Gary. Clearly, they were uninvited, but if the guests were happy, Lady Watterly seemed to be happy.

Relieved, Peep landed on Code's shoulder and refused to leave his side for the rest of the trip.

Outside the safely sealed window, the docking gates of the Celestial City appeared. Below them, Mekhos had shrunk to a grey green orb. Gary looked up from his oil of vitriol and wiped his face. "Are we there yet?" he asked.

Code smiled at Gary. He had thought the slaughterbot was helpless, but Gary had saved his life twice in the last few hours. The big clunky robot was cleverer than Code gave him credit for. Code was thankful to have made it up the Beamstalk at last—despite nearly being burned by acid, deprived of oxygen and bruised from a series of hearty thumps to the back from his new entourage of female robot admirers.

"We're here, Gary," said Code. "We're finally here."

16

Celestial City

The Great Disassembly:
T–Minus One Hour

Leaving behind the wild dinner party, Code and Gary crept unnoticed down a long, dark passageway of perfectly polished silver and into the Celestial City. With the Disassembly imminent, the city seemed completely empty. The only faces Code saw were the hologrammatic portraits of strange-looking humans that lined the walls—the past kings and queens of Mekhos, he assumed.

Code wondered whether he was related to any of these odd faces. Every single royal had some kind of robotic addition: a beautiful princess possessed piercing red robotic eyes, a rugged prince had two monstrous metal arms and in one particularly disturbing case, a haggard king was missing his lower half and instead stood proudly on eight golden spider legs. Code touched his own face thoughtfully. *Is this what's in store for me?*

Peep wriggled out of Code's pocket. She launched into

the air and purposefully buzzed ahead. As usual, Code and Gary followed close behind.

Passing through a low archway, Code emerged from the claustrophobic hall and entered the broad main street of the Celestial City. It was a vista that could only have been built by the peculiar robotic residents of Mekhos. Soaring turrets and towering walls crowded the sky under a vast translucent dome that twinkled with starlight. Rocket-powered elevators shot up and down the sheer faces of empty buildings. Stairways circled and squared their way around the streets and buildings, with some steps large enough for giants and others small enough for ants. It was incredible, but Code didn't have time to linger; he had to rush to catch up with Peep.

They trotted across empty pavilions and down deserted alleys. The city was eerily silent, except for the sharp snapping of banners in the artificial wind and the soft roar of waterfalls cascading beneath tall bridges. Ahead, the Celestial Castle was sprawling and magnificent—and deserted.

Finally, Peep led Code and Gary through a nondescript door and into the castle. Code had never seen her in such a rush. She peeped and blinked urgently as they trooped through cramped halls, winding their way deeper and deeper inside.

In the heart of the castle, the group reached a door covered in strong rivets and bands of thick metal. A dial illuminated with symbols protruded from the portal—a lock.

Below it, a confusing array of keys protruded from a panel, each a unique shape.

"A keyboard," whispered Gary.

Peep got busy. She hit the dial with a series of light beams and tugged on the keys one at a time. The dial spun and the keys shifted. And . . . nothing happened. Peep chirped in frustration.

"Oh, no!" cried Gary. "It's locked and we haven't got the combination."

In disbelief, Code stared down at the rows of keys. *It can't come down to this*, he thought. *There's got to be a way.* Leaning forward, Code looked closer at the keys. And closer. His grey green robo-retinas zoomed in until the confusing array of keys filled his vision. And he noticed something. Out of dozens, three of the keys were worn down slightly more than the others. It was a difference of just a few millimetres, but it was enough. Someone had touched these three keys more than the rest.

"Ah ha!" exclaimed Code, turning the three special keys in every combination he could think of. After a couple of tries, the lock opened with a thundering boom.

The impassable portal slid back, leaving behind a flurry of glimmering dust motes.

For a moment, Code thought the vast room inside was a burning inferno. Then he realised that the searing light wasn't caused by flames, but by the reflections of billions of coins, gems, artefacts, vehicles, weapons, armour, crowns, artwork, cannons and mysterious antiquities heaped into careless mounds between towering, gleaming archways. It was a treasure room beyond all measurement or comparison.

Code dimmed his robo-retinas and stumbled inside, craning his neck to inspect all the amazing treasures. Hovering orbs dotted the room, sending rays of luminescence cascading over the loot. Precarious piles of coins were heaped everywhere: tiny diamond coins, pie-sized golden coins, coins with legs crawling over each other and coins that dissolved together and spread apart like amoebas. Every coin was imprinted with the noble visage of King John Lightfall. An exoskeleton the size of a small building stood motionless on the far wall, its hands resting on a monumental sword.

Gary tromped around the room randomly, tossing up handfuls of coins and cackling with glee. Meanwhile, Code remained where he was and scanned the space carefully. He noticed that most of the brightly burning light converged on one spot at the far end of the room: a magnificent pedestal with a glass case on top.

At last, thought Code. *This must be where the Robonomicon is kept.* Code had imagined how the book would look: massive, dusty and covered in specks of gold. It would glitter in the light, and when he opened it, the writing would be in glimmering golden letters and filled with diagrams, maps and magical words—and all the answers he needed to save this world.

Code stumbled towards the pedestal like a sleepwalker, climbing over a half-buried aeroplane with the word "Electra" painted on its fuselage. Slipping on piles of coins, Code made his way up a mountain of loot and finally reached the glittering pedestal. Peep hovered near his head, tugging on his hair and fluttering at his ears. Code brushed her away and grabbed hold of the pedestal.

"I found it," he breathed.

"The Robonomicon?" asked Gary.

"Yes. We're saved, Gary."

Peep chirped frantically and shot beams of red light at Code. She yanked on his earlobe and smacked into his cheek. Mesmerised by the pedestal, Code paid no attention.

"Hooray!" thundered Gary.

Holding his breath with anticipation, Code yanked opened the case.

There was nothing inside but a cushioned pillow. The case was empty.

"Oh, no!" cried Code in despair.

"You got that right," said Gary.

Code turned and saw Immortalis hovering in the air like a robotic jellyfish. Two silent jet thrusters spit blue flame from either side of a writhing mass of black tentacles. The body of King John Lightfall dangled in the air, supported by hundreds of tentacles wrapped around his torso, arms, legs, head, feet and even his fingers. The cables twisted and wrinkled his elegant, kingly robes and he swung lightly.

A single unblinking blue eye adorned the middle of the Immortalis machine, like a glowing sapphire in a black crown.

Frightened, Peep alighted on Code's shoulder and hid under his collar.

Code's eyes widened as he met the gaze of his poor grandfather, caught in the foul embrace of Immortalis.

"My boy," uttered King John Lightfall. "Protect—"

The king's words were cut off as several thin black cords shot out of Immortalis and wrapped around his neck, jaw and face. A thicker cord tightened around his chest. The swiftly moving cords paused, then began moving together purposefully. Code grimaced as Immortalis played the king's tortured body like a puppet.

"Let him go, Immortalis!" demanded Code.

"*I* am King John Lightfall," hissed the old man in a wheezing grunt. His eyes rolled wildly. "And you are *too late.*"

A taut cord easily subdued a kick as John Lightfall tried to wriggle free of Immortalis.

"I made it this far, Immortalis," said Code. "Now where's the Robonomicon?"

"It's gone, gone, gone. And without her not even *you* can stop me, human," said John Lightfall.

Code could feel Peep under his shirt collar, trembling in fear. Alas, before he could stop her, the little bot bolted away and sped through the cavernous treasure room, ducking and weaving.

"Thank goodness!" said the king, in his own voice. Then the wires snapped his jaw shut and began moving his mouth again. "You!" he spat in a strangled voice, pointing at Peep.

Peep flew low over the mounds of treasure, a rapidly moving violet speck easily visible to Code's new eyes. He splashed after her through piles of coins, trying to protect the scared little robot from the black-tentacled monster. He finally caught up to her.

"What is it, Peep?" he implored. Immortalis was close behind.

Peep sprayed frantic light beams on to a small, humming box. It looked like a birthday present wrapped in smiley-face paper. A single button protruded from the top, serving double duty as the nose for a grinning happy face.

Immortalis shot out a half dozen tentacles towards Code. They wriggled across the coins like snakes. Every instinct Code had was shouting at him to run away, but he chose to trust the little robot.

Peep had never once led him astray.

Code jammed his finger on the button. Impossibly, the box folded in on itself until—somehow—it was no longer there. Instead, Code was surprised to see a boxy, friendly robot looking up at him, a paintbrush in its clawed hand.

"In the name of our ancestors! What have you done?!" cried the king, shrinking away. The happy little bot threw back its head and let out a psychotic laugh that sent a chill down Code's spine. Out of nowhere, Gary flopped his massive body down on to the mound of coins next to Code, then leaped to his feet.

"It's Charlie! The greatest robot hero in Mekhos history!"

"And criminal," muttered Code, backing away.

Without hesitation, Charlie wheeled over to an oddly curved black bar resting against an Egyptian sarcophagus. The bar was long and thin and it looked somehow dangerous. Charlie snatched it up, and with a sigh of satisfaction he cocked the bizarre weapon.

Just then, Immortalis descended on its jet thrusters in a roaring whirlwind of melting coins and let its tentacles fall like the branches of a weeping willow over the little square-shaped robot. Charlie fired his weapon three times, quickly. A tight beam of light vaporised a wriggling chunk of tentacle. Immortalis squealed in pain and retracted its tentacles, dropping King Lightfall. With a surprised expression on his face, the elderly king rolled out of reach of the hovering machine and on to a jingling bed of golden coins.

Peep chirped in distress. She fluttered over to the fallen king, landing on his chest. Code crouched down next to his injured grandfather.

Meanwhile, Immortalis soared up into the air, ignoring Code as it tried to escape from the plucky little robot with the big gun.

"Finally free," said the old man.

"Grandpa? Are you OK?" asked Code.

"Not really," chuckled the king. He managed to sit up on

one elbow, but collapsed back on the ground. Finally, he managed to say, "Oh, Code, you've grown up so much. This little one must have found you."

The king stroked Peep with one weak finger.

"You've been gone so long, Grandpa. Everyone thought you were dead. But I didn't believe them. I *never* believed them," said Code.

The old man now lying on the bed of gold coins had taught Code how to catch grasshoppers and how to pick out fossils from beds of shale rock. He was the only adult Code had ever known who didn't care about getting dirty, or looking silly, or being on time. And he was dying.

Code could feel each second of his grandfather's life ticking away, precious and irreplaceable. There were too many questions and not enough time.

"How did you get here? Why did this happen?" Code asked.

"Our ancestors built this place. One day it called to me. I was needed and so I came. Just as you did." After a fit of coughing, the king continued. "I feel like I've been here a thousand years, and yet you're still a boy. Time passes quickly here in Mekhos. Now it's all about to end."

"No, I can help. I can save Mekhos," said Code.

The king looked closely at his grandson. "Your eyes," he said sadly. "It's already beginning."

"Please," begged Code. "We have to stop the Disassembly.

This world will die. My friends will die. Tell me what to do. Please tell me how to find the Robonomicon."

The king smiled, his unseeing eyes staring vacantly into space. "Knowledge is worthless without action, Code. The Robonomicon can't help you if you don't help yourself."

Code sat back, confused. His grandfather stroked Peep affectionately. "Your little friend here is a queen, did you know that? She didn't let us down, did she?"

"Grandpa," said Code. "Please . . ."

The king grimaced in pain. "I'm afraid that I've reached the end of my program, Code. But the story of Mekhos isn't over. Your time here has just begun."

Peep purred as she rubbed against the dying king's cheek.

"Wait," said Code. "You can't die! I came such a long way, but I still don't know how to save Mekhos. I don't know what you mean about helping myself. The Robonomicon has all the answers, not *me*," said Code. "I don't understand anything!"

The king took Code by the hand and looked into his eyes. "You're doing fine. Just finish it and begin again." And with a loving smile, the king whispered, "I'm proud of you, Code. You're a good boy. A prince."

Then the old man closed his eyes and stopped breathing. With a last flash of tender blue light at the fallen king, Peep fluttered into the air and disappeared into Code's shirt pocket. Code could feel the tiny bot sobbing against his chest.

I can't believe he's gone, thought Code. He had come all this way to find his grandfather, and then he couldn't even find a way to save the old man. The Disassembly was about to happen, he never found the Robonomicon, and he had let loose a crazed robot. Even worse . . . Immortalis. Code was trapped in a room with a killer machine—

Suddenly, a lethal beam of energy shot past and liquefied the top layer of coins a few feet from where Code crouched. Gary sprayed coins as he rolled violently out of the way. "Code! I think it's time to make our move."

Code looked up just in time to see Charlie, cackling madly, fire two colossal shots from his flaming weapon. Immortalis dodged and the blazing beams of light vaporised two ragged holes the size of swimming pools in the ceiling. Gary murmured in appreciation as Charlie finished by burning a smile just beneath the two eyeholes. Above them, the smiley face had penetrated multiple levels of the castle and obliterated the outside dome.

Code screamed as Celestial City's air supply began to rush out of the gaping holes in the translucent dome above. The entire city tilted violently. Lights and alarms blared and buzzed. A reassuring mechanical voice announced that it was time to board the escape pods.

Code took one last look at the body of his beloved

grandfather before Gary reached down and tucked him under one arm. Carrying Code, the robot lumbered out of the door in search of the escape pods.

Nobody noticed Immortalis, who was in close pursuit of the only remaining human being in Mekhos.

17

Slidecar

The Great Disassembly:
T–Minus Fifteen Minutes

Minutes later, Code, Gary and Peep sat catching their breaths in a bean-shaped escape pod. The pod careened down the Beamstalk and away from the falling Celestial City. Hundreds of other pods slid down the wildly swinging Beamstalk towards the roof of the Monolith Building below. As it dropped, their escape craft spoke.

"Whew!" it exclaimed. "I thought this day would never come. I've been trained and trained, but I never get to *do* anything. And now here it is, my big moment!"

"That's nice," replied Code.

"Yeah," said the pod. "I'm really excited."

"My grandpa is gone," said Code. "All of you robots are going to be disassembled in a little less than twenty minutes. And it's my fault."

Code couldn't even look Gary in the battle visor, afraid

of what he might see there. This entire world was crumbling around them and he'd done nothing to stop it.

The pod sighed theatrically. "That's really ... yeah ... not good. But how am I doing? Is your ride smooth? I recently received an upgrade to help reduce turbulence. It's awfully exciting. So I really want to know. Is this going well for you?"

Overwhelmed, Code buried his face into the crook of his elbow. Peep nuzzled Code's neck. Gary glared out of the window, cracking his finger cannons one by one.

"You know what?" murmured the pod. "I'm going to take that as a yes."

Finally, the escape pod touched down on the wide, flat roof of the Monolith Building. Code and Gary hurried out of the door and into total chaos. In the sky, huge shards of the destroyed city were flaming down. Massive chunks of debris smashed into the plains below and sizzled into the Fomorian Sea beyond.

The escape pod called out to them. "On a scale from one to ten——"

Just then, a chunk of fiery rock smashed through the roof of the pod, filling it with smoke and sparks.

"We have to get out of here," Code whispered to Gary.

In the sky, the Celestial City glowed a fiery orange as it plunged through the upper atmosphere. The wind ripped at Code's clothes. He covered his ears to dampen the shrieking noise of falling debris. He could feel the reassuring weight of Peep as she burrowed deep into his shirt pocket.

Above, hundreds more escape pods slid down the wavering Beamstalk. As Code watched in horror, the Beamstalk made an awful hissing noise, flickered and snapped out of existence. As if in slow motion, escape pods scattered across the sky like pearls flung off a broken necklace.

A handful of straggling robots hurried past Code, chattering to each other. "At this rate, we'll never even make it down to Disassembly Point to be properly disassembled!" one of them exclaimed.

Peep fluttered out of Code's pocket and shot an angry light beam at the boy's face. He tore his gaze from the sky and noticed a row of sleek, low slidecars painted in a rainbow of colours. Each slidecar was repeating in a robotic voice: "Emergency! Impact detected. Free-ride mode initiated. Please board and survive. Have a good day!"

Code looked down at the feisty little robot. Certain death had never seemed so certain, *but if Peep is still willing to fight, then so am I*, he thought.

"Let's go!" Code called through the wind. He raced to the nearest slidecar and the door automatically popped open. He threw himself inside and hunched forward as Gary crammed his bulky frame into the vehicle. The door snapped shut. Code sat in the driver's seat for a moment, stunned by the sudden silence. Outside, a hailstorm of wreckage continued to rain down. Then Peep viciously pinched Code on the arm.

"Car! Go!" he commanded.

The slidecar replied, "Welcome to the Monolith Community Slideracer. Please assume control now. Drive and survive! Have a good day!"

A steering wheel popped out of the dash and nudged Code in the rib cage. A five-point harness whipped out and snugly wrapped around Code's chest, slapping him briskly across the cheek.

"Punch it, Code," urged Gary.

Rubbing his cheek, Code muttered, "But I don't even know how to drive yet."

Peep chirped fearfully and bounced purple light against the roof window of the slidecar. Code looked up just in time to see a chunk of burning infrastructure roar past the Monolith Building. High above, the main body of the castle was breaking up into slowly rotating pieces and the debris was headed straight for them.

Code stopped thinking. He gunned what he assumed was the accelerator pad and jammed a stick down. The ultralight slidecar sped forward. Gary cheered wildly. But his cheer turned into a shout of fear when the car flew directly over the side of the building. They hung in the air for an agonising few seconds, and then the gravthrusters kicked in. Instead of falling, the slidecar stuck to the side of the building, pointing straight towards the ground.

The slidecar raced down along the ebony face of the Monolith Building, speeding past plunging exterior elevators, other skidding slidecars and heaps of falling rubble. Unfortunately, Code failed to notice the plodding approach of a window cleaner with sucker feet attached to legs the size of redwood trees. The cleaner, named Terrance, did spot the oncoming vehicle, but having already made the decision to continue cleaning windows right up until the moment of Disassembly, opted not to change course for something as insignificant as a small, out-of-control slidecar.

They were on an unavoidable crash course with the window cleaner.

At five seconds to impact—well past the point of no return—Gary helpfully mentioned, "We're on an unavoidable crash course with that window cleaner!"

The slidecar, however, was designed to be not only fast but safe. It was a happy surprise to Code when the slidecar seats automatically ejected into the air a moment before impact and he and his friends parachuted safely to the ground. As Code shouted in joy at being alive, Peep glowed a sad violet and chirped at the poor destroyed slidecar.

Terrance paused, mildly disappointed and then continued cleaning the soon-to-be-shattered windows.

18

The Great Disassembly

The Great Disassembly:
T–Minus One Minute

At the base of the Monolith, Code and Gary stood up, dusted themselves off and detached their parachutes. The Fomorian Sea had swallowed the last of the Celestial City. All around them, across the bleak plain of the Right Eyeland, millions of robots stood in absolute silence, waiting.

As Gary and Code approached the huge crowd of robots that were standing a safe distance from the Monolith, Peep suddenly darted out of Code's pocket.

"Wait!" shouted Code.

But she was off in a flash. The brightly glowing green speck disappeared into endless ranks of robots, spraying emerald light beams in every direction. Code could do nothing but blink in surprise. Peep was gone. Code looked up at Gary, but the big robot just shook his head sadly.

In the moment before the Disassembly, there was no

blinking, no movement and no conversation. Every formation was complete, every goodbye already said and every robot prepared to march into certain death. The lonely gong of a clock rang out, and just like that—perfectly on time— the Disassembly began.

Code felt a sudden electric change go through his body. It was as though lightning were about to strike. The hairs on the back of his neck stood up as a low moaning sound rose up, caused by the wind rushing towards the centre of the great plain. Clouds were gathering above the stark black Monolith Building, turning an ominous shade of greenish yellow.

Like row upon row of statues, the massive horde of robots stood perfectly still and watched the sky. Reflections of purple lightning flickered from the robots' metal skin as, high above, a churning hole appeared in the boiling clouds. For a split second, blue sky shone through the hole. It felt to Code as though the scene were frozen in time—as if the world had stopped spinning on its axis.

Then a whirling funnel of clouds formed, reaching down and engulfing the Monolith Building. As the dark clouds spun around it, small black pieces of the building began to break away. Each cube-shaped piece was swept away and up, higher and higher, to where it disappeared in the rumbling clouds above.

The Great Disassembly had arrived.

Code watched in awe as the massive funnel lowered over the Monolith Building, disintegrating the mile-high tower piece by piece. The swirling storm clouds were soon stained black with debris. When the funnel finally touched down, a torrent of brown dust lifted up from the plain and climbed into the sky.

The Monolith Building was gone and, worse, the robots were beginning to walk towards the funnel. They walked together in hundreds of neat lines that snaked across the plain, politely tromping towards the storm. A hundred-foot-tall stilt-legged walker swayed unsteadily over the crowds, then pitched forward and disappeared into the dark funnel. Swarms of insects buzzed overhead and were pulled into the twisting vortex. Robot giants, ladybots and even the infinipede marched in an orderly fashion into the heart of the rotating storm.

As each robot got near, the screaming wind swept it up into the air, where it was disassembled into parts and then into smaller parts and finally into a fine, metallic sand. The storm swallowed every robot that came near.

Speechless, Code watched the Disassembly unfold. To his surprise, the robots did not seem afraid, but Code was still dismayed to see destruction on such a massive scale. The unique beauty of Mekhos was being extinguished. And it was all because Code hadn't found the Robonomicon in time.

Then things got infinitely worse: Gary began to walk towards the mayhem.

"Gary, no!" pleaded Code. "I'll protect you."

"It's OK, Code. I'm not afraid. Each of us has to follow our own programming."

"But it doesn't make any sense!"

"I know. Sometimes things don't make sense. It's like when you humans fall asleep at night. It's such a silly thing. But when it gets late, your eyes start to close . . . There's nothing to be done."

Code couldn't bear to see his friend disassembled. After travelling all the way across Mekhos, it was unthinkable that they could fail now. There had to be some way out of this. But the Disassembly was here—it was happening right now.

Desperate, Code grabbed Gary by the leg and held on tight.

"I won't let you go," said Code.

Gary looked down at Code fondly. "It was you, Code, a delicate little human, who showed me how to be brave. You taught me that each of us must face our destiny—even if the outcome is uncertain. It's better to do something than to do nothing at all."

Gary put one razor-sharp gauntlet on Code's shoulder and gently pushed him away. "Code, thank you for coming with me to the Disassembly. I'm sorry that we didn't find the Robonomicon, but I had a really fun time looking for it. We did our best."

"Gary, please," said Code. "You're my best friend."

"Goodbye, little buddy," Gary said sadly.

Code watched helplessly as Gary turned and lumbered

away for the last time. The mighty slaughterbot built up speed and stormed across the chaotic plain. The tornado of destruction swirled, massive and unstoppable, sending up a billowing wall of disintegrated metal, plastic and glass.

Gary was headed straight for it.

"No!" shouted Code.

But it was too late.

With a fearsome battle cry Gary charged into the swirling mass of destruction. The metallic bulk of Gary's armoured body was swept away into the maelstrom. Nothing was left behind but scoured earth.

Code squeezed his eyes shut and fell to his knees. When he could bear to look again, the dust was clearing on the plain. All that was visible was scoured rock. Particles of metallic sand drifted gently down like snow, glittering silently. The storm was over. Code stood all by himself on the empty, barren rock plain.

"Oh, no," sobbed Code. He buried his face in his hands. Hot tears coursed down his cheeks. Peep and Gary had gone and left him alone.

There was no more movement, no more sound. The entire robot population of Mekhos had been disassembled into dust-sized parts. Above, the sunlight shimmered from the swirling metallic sand that had been created by the Disassembly.

If any of the robots had been alive to see the utter destruction of Mekhos, they would have been very, very proud. The

Great Disassembly had been the single most complicated feat of robots in the history of Mekhos. In one hour, the entire population had pulled off a coordinated exercise in which every member had shown up, been accounted for and been disassembled. And they had done it without any errors, delays, or accidental survivors.

Except for one, that is.

19

Robonomicon

Peep!

Code felt a small weight on his shoulder. For a few long seconds, he was unable to drag his eyes away from the horribly empty plain. Then it dawned on him: Peep was still alive! He turned his head to see her. Covered in dust and soot, she wearily clambered in a small circle and sat down on Code's shoulder. For the first time since they'd met, Peep did not shoot a beam of light at anything or dart away to inspect something. There was nothing to memorise or record—no robots, no schematics and no order.

Suddenly, Code cried out in pain as something wrapped tightly around his thigh. He grabbed it with both hands but couldn't budge it. Looking down, Code saw a leathery black tentacle.

"The rifts are open!" said a monstrous voice.

"Immortalis?" said Code, bewildered.

Code clasped Peep in his hands tightly as another tendril snaked around his upper arm. With its blue eye glowing malevolently, Immortalis lifted Code into the air and pulled him close.

"But why are you still here?" Code gasped.

Using a flurry of small tentacles, Immortalis drummed out a sound on the top of its frame. In soft, musical notes, the machine hissed, "*You* saved me, young King Lightfall. My instructions are to protect the human king. So long as I have you, I do not have to follow the others. You are mine, human. We will rebuild this world as we wish. And then we will cross the rift and enter your world as conquerors! Now give me the Robonomicon."

"Robonomicon? I don't have it. I never even found it," said Code, ashamed.

"What a fool you are! The recorder. The one you call Peep. She *is* the Robonomicon."

The information hit Code like a shock wave. Peep was the Robonomicon? But then he remembered how Peep had shone a beam of light on everything—the infinipede, the armoured insects, the giants, the slaughterbot, the nanobots . . . everything and everyone. Scanning them . . . *recording* them. His little friend had always known where to go and how to get there. And the king: Peep had known who he was. It was like they were old friends. Code looked down at his clenched fist and remembered what Gary had said so long ago: *She is very small. You should protect her.*

Immortalis laughed—an oddly beautiful sound, like a waterfall of coins falling into a well. "When John Lightfall realised what I had become and what I intended to do, he spirited her away and set her free. I can only imagine that he sent her to find *you*, thinking he could save himself. She recorded every creature you met, every place you visited and so much more. Even during the Disassembly she memorised every individual automaton in our world. And after all that, you still *failed*. With her knowledge we will cross between worlds at will, building an army fit to shatter the universe! Our dominion will spread to the ends of reality, and it will last for ever."

Code shook his head, clasping Peep tightly in his fist. Immortalis could never be allowed to have such strength. And despite her incredible power, Peep was his last and only friend. He refused to give her up. The twisting appendages tightened across Code's body, crushing the breath out of his lungs. They lifted him high and swung him in a gut-wrenching circle.

"You have no choice," said Immortalis.

The Robonomicon has been with me this whole time, thought Code. *And I didn't realise it in time to save Gary. Or my grandfather.*

Code slumped in despair.

"Now you understand," said Immortalis. "She knows everything. She *is* everything. And now she is mine."

"No—" Code was cut off by a fast-tightening cord wrapped around his chest. He struggled frantically, but each movement only trapped him more. A flurry of small thread-like tentacles reached for his mouth, prising open his sealed lips and grasping his tongue and jaw. Against his will, Code was forced to speak: "We. Are. Code. Imm— Immortalis."

"That's better," said Immortalis. "Your body is young. In my embrace you will live many thousands of years. We will rule this world and many others. With the Robonomicon, our power will be limitless."

Peep shivered in Code's palm, terrified. Unable to move his head, Code rolled his eyes to see her. The coils were too strong to resist. Immortalis was ancient and confident, unstoppable. Code could already imagine his future, bleak and inevitable. He was to be a puppet, forced to ride along as Immortalis corrupted Mekhos and more, committing crime after unthinkable crime. He simply could not think of anything more to do. *Maybe*, thought Code, *it's finally time that I just do nothing.*

As if sensing Code's despair, Immortalis relaxed its grip.

"Yes," it purred. "There is no escape. Give her to me."

Code raised his clenched fist upwards and slowly opened his palm. For one split second, Peep stood exposed and unprotected. She looked at Code, uncomprehending. The most powerful artefact in all of Mekhos sat completely vulnerable in Code's pale, quivering palm.

"I'm sorry, Peep, but I've had enough," said Code. Staring defiantly into the sapphire eye of Immortalis, he said, "You can have her, Immortalis—but you'll have to kill me first!"

Roaring in anger, Immortalis sent a flurry of manipulator tentacles dashing towards the little winged robot. And then Code did something unexpected—he stuffed Peep into his mouth and swallowed her whole. It was the only way he could think of to protect her.

Immortalis stopped. Its azure eye blinked, puzzled. Then a cascade of tentacles crashed against its frame, creating a loud and long wail of fury.

The hovering machine folded Code's body into the centre of its oval frame and yanked his arms and legs until they were fully outstretched. More tentacles wrapped around his torso and writhed back and forth, squeezing, grinding, crushing. Code dangled spread-eagle, suspended and helpless as the machine's infinite tentacles encircled his arms, legs, fingers and face.

"I will tear you to pieces. My many arms will sift through your guts until I find her," the machine threatened. "When I have the Robonomicon, you will be dead and I will rule this ruined world, for ever and ever and ever. And one day, another human will come through the rift and I will be *free*."

Against his will, Code's arms were forced into a dance posture. The flying machine began to waltz through the air over the destroyed landscape, moving Code's arms and legs in a gross parody of a dance. Covered in black wires, Code could only grunt in frustration as the machine forced him through the motions.

But a silent battle raged inside of Code's body and mind.

Code had swallowed the Robonomicon. Although he had no idea, Peep was much more than a simple flying robot. With all the knowledge of Mekhos at her disposal, she was a wise and powerful queen.

Peep had never before explored the interior landscape of a human body, but she was a fast learner. Within a few beats of Code's heart, she had spread herself to every part of his body. Atom by atom, Peep converted Code's organic body into inorganic material.

In a matter of seconds, Code's transformation into a citizen of Mekhos was complete. Peep had replaced every atom of Code's body. And although he looked the same, Code found that he was no longer human.

Code took a gasping, shuddering breath and pulled his arms down to his sides. Motors squealed as Immortalis strained against Code's newfound strength. Immortalis blinked its blue eye once. Then twice. Processing.

Code's shoes began to dissolve and disappear.

Immortalis made an alarmed screech. It retracted its tentacles and dropped Code like a poisonous snake. Code cartwheeled through the air, smashed to the ground and plunged several feet into solid stone. He rolled on to his back. The rock melted wherever he touched it. His flickering grey green eyes opened and they stared straight up, unseeing.

Code felt the strangest tickling sensation all through his body. He could feel the stone around him being broken down at an atomic level and pulled into his skin. *Castle walls*, he thought. *Peep is using the rock to build castle walls inside me.*

Immortalis hurled a wicked-looking primary harpoon tentacle towards Code. Before it could connect, Code's skin solidified into a hexagon of solid, glinting stone. The tip of the tentacle hit the stone and shattered in a spray of rock dust and sparks.

Immortalis screeched in pain and retracted its mangled tentacle. The machine bellowed angrily. Thousands of tentacles peeled away from the black frame: tree-trunk-thick primaries, whip-like secondaries and toothy tertiaries, armed with all manner of weapons, dripping with poisons and humming with energy. The metallic tentacles rose in all directions, writhing in anticipation of all-out attack.

"Cower!" boomed Immortalis. "Beg for mercy."

Code stood up. The small, pale boy walked unsteadily towards the hovering monster. Each step he took left a deep footprint in the rocky ground. Somehow, Peep was absorbing everything Code touched and using it to build armour. He felt strong and full of potential, almost invincible.

Without hesitation, Immortalis unleashed a storm of tentacles. Searing energy bursts showered over Code as thick attack cables with flexing razors and spinning blades burst into flames upon touching his skin. With a wave of his hand, Code severed the Mainline thrust cable as it swung towards his head like an out-of-control crane. Every surface of Code's body sprayed dust and energy and heat as the tentacles crashed against him again and again.

Four primary tentacles snaked low over the ground and snatched Code by the legs, sweeping him into the air. Without access to the stone underfoot, Code's armour began to weaken. Hundreds, then thousands of tentacles crashed and broke against Code's body, like waves on a shore. At last, one serrated-blade tentacle sliced a deep gash in Code's face and he began to bleed. Immortalis cackled in delight and waved its few remaining tentacles in victory as blood dripped down Code's face.

"The human is broken! Mastered! My puppet for ever!" howled Immortalis. The machine tilted and floated in a slow circle. It held Code suspended overhead, looking up at him with a sapphire eye that glowed white blue with triumph.

Code looked down at Immortalis sadly, drops of his blood pattering down on to the machine.

"I'm sorry for you," said Code, for he understood his sudden surge of strength. Like the kings and queens of Mekhos before him, Code had made a transformation. He and Peep were one and the same now.

The blood dripping from Code's wounds was no longer human. Peep had spread throughout Code's body and defended it and made it strong—and she was in his blood now. Code thought of his own narrow escape from the inky black pool of nanobots in the Nanoscopic Traverse as he watched his blood spatter on to Immortalis.

Suddenly, the machine cried out in confusion and fright as each drop of blood dissolved through its tentacles, warping its frame. The toxic blood spread over Immortalis, eating through its skin like acid. The beastly machine was unable to comprehend how a defenceless little boy could have dealt such a devastating blow.

Trailing smoke, Immortalis dropped from the sky. Foul vapour poured from the machine as it smashed on to the plain, hugging Code's body in a death embrace. Its panicked screams soon diminished, reduced to the random beating of tentacles spasming against the ground. Code's body was swallowed by the wreckage of the machine. For long moments, nothing moved.

Finally, Code crawled out of the smoking crater. There was nothing left of Immortalis but its lone blue eye and several tiny vibrating tentacles, like harmless bird feathers. As the sapphire eye faltered, faded and blinked, the delicate appendages tapped out a last message: "Error. Error. Err—"

20

Reset

Code looked at the annihilated surface of Mekhos and saw only a primordial sea of wreckage swirling in a formless, meaningless void. Billowing clouds of atomised matter blocked the rays of the sun and moon. Nothing changed, nothing lived and nothing died. Mekhos was gone.

The only trace of the robots that had once lived here were now trapped inside Code's body—a part of him. *It's finally happened*, he thought. *I've gone all the way and become one of them.* Code looked at the strange shimmering skin of his hands. *I'm the last robot left in Mekhos*, he thought sadly. *And now I can never go home.*

But in his heart, Code still wondered if something, somewhere, might still live. Maybe deep down in the crushing depths of the sea, or above in the highest stratosphere of the air?

He walked to the edge of the island. The sea below

frothed and boiled in confusion. Code thought about swimming. With a little concentration, he found that he was able to convince his body to *transform*. His legs quivered, then fused together and extended into a long silver tail. Code pulled his arms in close to his body until they melded into his skin. His elbows flattened and collapsed into the shape of wide, powerful fins. The transformation complete, he allowed himself to fall into the frothing sea below.

Once in the water, Code's body rearranged itself until he could not feel the numbing coldness or the crushing pressure. His eyes grew to the size of saucers, until he could see for miles in utter darkness. He felt no need to take just one shape and so he adopted whichever one worked best. But search as he might, Code found nothing in the fathomless depths. Not a single creature, large or small, stirred in the deep. The black water was empty and devoid of life.

Rising from the water, Code leaped into the sky and arched his back, sprouting a pair of great shining wings. Flapping his nearly translucent metal wings, he searched for life in the skies. But as he swooped through the heavens, he saw only the cold light of the moon playing out random, senseless patterns on the shattered wreckage of Mekhos. Code sped through misty clouds and dived through crystal clear skies. But no creatures had survived to fly in the air, either.

Code was heartbroken. The robots had really done it. They had managed to completely remove themselves from the world. All the trees and the castles and rocks had been vaporised. From the tiniest microrobots to the biggest bron-tobots, all life had disappeared.

And the reality of Code's solitude began to set in.

The world was empty. The seas had boiled. The Odd Woods were disintegrated. Clockwork City was obliterated. All inhabitants of the land had been eradicated: the impatient, endless infinipede; the angry robot giants in their crystalline castles; the hungry Toparian mowers; the countless tiny peoples of the arid Nanoscopic Traverse; Charlie, the greatest robot hero in Mekhos; and the pompous Lady Watterly and her chatty guests. Even Gary and Peep had met their ends. They were all gone. Destroyed for ever.

Code rose higher and higher in the air, trying to escape from the loneliness that haunted the ghost world below. The rising sun painted a crescent of dawn along the eastern curve of the world. Floating above the devastation, in dark-ness and ruin, Code felt an overwhelming sadness.

And as he thought about his friends and the places he had seen and the adventures they'd had together, Code's nose began to sting, his cheeks turned red and his lip began to quiver.

And since there was nobody around to see or hear, he began to cry.

A drop of liquid coursed down his cheek and dan-gled from his jawline. After a moment, it fell. The wind whipped that single tear into innumerable invisible droplets and spread those specks of moisture over many miles. Those millions of water molecules landed randomly on the rich primordial soil of Mekhos.

And something interesting began to happen.

Where each tear landed, the ground began to move. Each drop was filled with the memory of cities, nations and kingdoms of robots. And everywhere they landed, the tears began to convert the raw clay of the nothing into . . . *something*. Within seconds, all across Mekhos, magnificent creatures—titans—began to rise up from the ground. Huge and not very bright, the titans rose up and looked into the sky, where Code hung like a shining star. They saw that much work needed to be done.

Code thought about what his grandfather had said: *Finish it, and begin again.*

And as Code watched these mountain-sized beings emerging from the smoke and ash below, a spark of hope flared in his chest. He found that when he thought about it, he knew the true name of every robot, large and small, in all of Mekhos.

As the titans set to work, Code began to recite each robot's name. He found that each name came out as a command, and the titans obeyed, using their rough, colossal hands to mould those creatures from dust. The titans worked ceaselessly, and over the course of their lifetimes a familiar bunch of robots crawled, leaped and slithered once again into Mekhos. The skies, lands and depths of the seas were soon teeming again with flying robot insects, shambling giants and armour-plated whales.

Mekhos erupted into life and activity. Hours later, an arc of light shot up from the ground directly below Code. A string of self-replicating nanobots raced upwards, re-creating the Beamstalk as they went. At the top of the string, a swirling cloud of nanobots formed itself into a castle-shaped mist that solidified into the seat of royal power—the Celestial City.

As he uttered each name, Code felt his power diminish. Eventually, his wings shrank and then faded away, and his small body floated down on to the vast promenade of the Celestial City. Behind him, a soft red carpet rolled over the cobblestone courtyard, leading across the plaza and up a wide staircase, ending at the foot of a towering silver throne.

Below, Mekhos was once again filled with everyday robots of all shapes and sizes, along with their Clockwork Cities and leaping transpeds and hologrammatic art and alien treasures.

And finally, the mighty titans collapsed in exhaustion, having finished their great tasks. A sand titan crashed to the ground and exploded into billions of nanoparticles, becoming the desert of the Nanoscopic Traverse; a tree titan lay down quietly and died, letting his rich corpse feed the verdant plants of the Toparian Wyldes; and a rock titan fell down and passed on, whereupon his bones became the crystalline castles of the robot giants.

It was done.

Mekhos was born anew. It spread as high as the wind blew and as deep as the sea currents ran. Code uttered one final name and felt the last of the Robonomicon's power ebb. His bare feet touched down on the cool stones of the viewing promenade. At last, Code Lightfall returned to being a normal boy. He collapsed on to the ground and drifted into the deepest sleep of his young life.

Just then, the ground beneath Code's sleeping body stirred and rumbled. A long, low chuckle echoed from the empty courtyard, and a razor-sharp spiked fist burst up out of the ground, spraying cobblestones. The fist was attached to an even bigger atomic slaughterbot. Gary rose to his feet and looked around. He looked the same as before the Disassembly, only now he was protected by shining white armour, and a majestic golden cape was slung over one hulking shoulder. Gary had been deactivated as a common slaughterbot and had returned as a royal knight.

When Gary saw his friend Code lying on the ground, he heaved a sad sigh and began to dig a boy-sized grave. But after a moment, he remembered a strange fact about how human beings often go unconscious. So he stopped digging, gently lifted the boy from the ground, and climbed the steps to the silver throne. Then he laid his sleeping friend on to the cushioned seat of royal power.

From inside the Celestial City, a distinguished group of robots solemnly walked into the courtyard. They wore splendid robes of white mesh and glowed with energy and power. Joining Gary, they formed a semicircle around the sleeping boy on the throne. In hushed tones, the robots began to discuss Code's fate.

"I propose we make him our king," said Lady Watterly. With extreme poise, she raised one arm, adding, "I shall teach him the necessary manners."

An elderly little robot repositioned its cracked spectacles. "Eh?! We need him full-time at the fabrication tank. The boy has a talent for making top-notch robots."

Gary blushed.

"Well, then who's going to judge our art contests?" demanded a crewbot wearing an immaculate sailor's outfit.

The group of robots burst into a heated discussion, full of interruptions, accusations and disruptions. Two mowers yapped at each other and a robot giant bellowed loudly, as an infinipede ran around everyone in circles—unable to stop.

Finally, a deep voice rang out.

"Enough!" thundered Gary. The other robots fell silent.

"Code journeyed across Mekhos for us. He battled Immortalis for us. And he survived the destruction of our world for us. When he could have given in to despair, Code fought on. For us. It is only fair that he should return home to his own world, while he still can. And if our friend Code Lightfall ever wishes to return to Mekhos, then we will see him again."

The other robots nodded to each other in agreement. Under the clear white starlight, they gathered shoulder to shoulder and watched over the sleeping boy. The decision had been made. And with that, Gary sat down on the steps to wait patiently for his dear friend to wake up.

21

Homecoming

With a start, Code opened his eyes. He was on his back, surrounded by tall tufts of grass. Sunlight filtered through oak trees overhead, dazzling his eyes. Something was very strange about this place. The leaves were ... moving. A breeze blew cool across his face, and Code felt the tickle of soft grass on his neck. *Real* grass.

This isn't right, he thought. *Unless ...*

Afraid to look, Code sat up. He was on Mek Mound. The storm had passed and the skies were clear. In the distance, he saw the bright yellow of the school bus. He could hear the other students talking to each other further down the hill. Mr Mefford was asking for their worksheets.

Oh, no, he thought. *It couldn't have been a dream.*

The other kids were assembling at the bottom of the

mound. Code noticed that the sun had moved across the sky, and he was suddenly feeling very hungry. Instinctively, he patted his shirt pocket.

Peep wasn't there.

Code grabbed a handful of grass and tore it from the ground. It was all just a dream?! But Peep had been his friend. And Gary. His grandfather. *I finally did something*, thought Code. *Instead of just thinking about it, I went out and risked my life. Or I thought I did. Was it in my imagination after all?*

Disappointed and confused, Code stood up and dusted himself off. He yawned and stretched. Without Peep's reassuring presence, he already felt a loneliness in the pit of his stomach.

And the worst part, he thought, *is that nobody will ever believe me.*

Code picked up his backpack and shuffled down the hill to join the class. The students were gathered around Mr Mefford as he collected the worksheets.

"Nice of you to join us, Code," said Mr Mefford. "Worksheet?"

Code patted his pockets. He didn't have the worksheet on him anywhere.

"I must have lost it," he said.

Mr Mefford frowned at Code. "Well, you'll have to make it up when we get back to school. Don't think you're off the hook."

Mr Mefford continued to collect worksheets from the other students. Code ran his fingers through his hair, in a daze. Where could his sheet have gone?

Tyler walked over to Code, a mean smirk on his face. With a bulging backpack slung over his shoulders, Tyler looked like an angry turtle. He snapped the shoulder straps together over his chest and the waist straps around his hips.

"Nice move, Code. I thought you were mister know-it-all?"

"It's not what I know, it's what I do," replied Code. And without thinking about it, he reached out and unsnapped Tyler's chest fastener, sending the heavy backpack flopping to the ground, the waist strap yanking Tyler's trousers down around his ankles.

Tyler yelped and tried to catch his bag and his trousers at the same time. But it was too late. Sylvia and Zachary giggled as Tyler staggered around, trying desperately to pull up his trousers. Code covered his mouth and tried not to laugh.

Mr Mefford noticed and put his hands on his hips.

"Stop clowning around," he said.

"Code did it," whined Tyler.

Mr Mefford looked at Code questioningly. Code shrugged, sheepish. Surprisingly, Mr Mefford winked at Code and stifled a small smile.

"Then you probably deserved it," he said, and then clapped his hands together. "Everybody on the bus! The field trip is over. Time to get back to school."

On the way to the bus, Code noticed Hazel looking at him curiously. He raised his eyebrows and looked back. And this time, neither one of them looked away.

"Hi," said Hazel.

Code blinked in surprise. Hazel hadn't said three words to him since second grade.

"Hi."

"You look different," she said. "Have your eyes always been that colour?"

Code touched his face. "Why? What colour are they?"

"Brown. I mean green. Grey? I don't know. I can't really describe it."

Code blinked again and then froze. His eyes had just taken a picture of Hazel. She stood framed by the massive mound, long, sunlit hair cascading over her shoulders and her eyes wide and curious—a question on her face. Clearing his vision, Code smiled at Hazel. "I suppose they must have changed," he said.

Perplexed, she gave him a half smile and swung her backpack on to one shoulder.

"Oh," she said. "Talk to you later, OK?"

Speechless, Code nodded, then watched her go.

A minute later, Code stepped on to the crowded school bus and sat down in the very last row. *The first row is safe*, he thought. *But the last row is more interesting.* As the bus pulled out of the parking lot, however, he began to feel very strange. His stomach made a worrisome gurgling sound. His nose twitched, his eyes jerked closed and he let out the biggest sneeze of his life.

At the end of this stupendous nasal explosion, something extraordinary happened—Peep fluttered out of Code's mouth. She buzzed happily against his face, then dived towards his book bag. While she flopped around inside, Code scanned the faces of the other students in microscopic detail to make sure no one had seen. They hadn't.

Looking down, he saw that Peep was tugging on a history book. Code took it out and set it on his lap. Flickering through the air, Peep pulled the book open and flipped pages. Finally, Peep settled herself on to a page and chirped urgently up at Code.

Code saw that Peep was sitting on the section about Mound Builders. On the page under her feet was a crude map, sprinkled with dots. It dawned on Code that each dot on the map represented another mound—there were dozens, all over the country.

"Oh, boy," muttered Code.

And before anyone could see, the ecstatic little bot darted straight into his shirt pocket. Code put one hand protectively over her and smiled to himself. It felt good to have the warm lump of metal over his heart again.

* * *

[Traverse Initiated]
[Three]
[Two]
[One]
[Activate]
[The End]

Acknowledgments

Many thanks to the people who helped this book along its circuitous path:

Members of the Big Brain Trust for reading drafts and providing feedback, sometimes on the stormy coast of Oregon: Marc Acito, Courtenay Hameister, Storm Large, Christine McKinley and Cynthia Whitcomb.

My editors at Bloomsbury, Melanie Cecka and Margaret Miller, for hanging on patiently while this book figured out what to be when it grew up.

My literary agent, Laurie Fox and manager, Justin Manask, for always bringing their A game.

Dan Stern for his etymological skills.

My wife, Anna, for pointing out the bad stuff before the good stuff.

And finally, my heartfelt thanks go out to everyone who visits Mekhos. Remember not to stay too long in the Toparian Wyldes, and try not to startle the atomic slaughterbots—they're more delicate than they look.